'You're so damned smart!' Sarah snapped.

'I'd say I need to be, with unsavoury characters like you around.'

'It takes one to know one, as they say.' She threw him a look of cold contempt. 'No doubt that sort of deviousness comes naturally to you.'

'And your prying nature seems admirably suited to your trade.'

She'd been half expecting that. 'A trade for which, I gather, you have little respect.'

'Not the trade,' Brett corrected her. 'Just some of the people who practise it.'

'What's the matter? Do you have so many secrets you need to hide?'

'If I do, you'll never uncover them.' He held her eyes. 'I don't leave them lying around in drawers.'

Exposed and suddenly embarrassed, she snatched her gaze away. 'I've already told you, what I did had nothing whatsoever to do with my work on the *Gazette*. And I've admitted it was wrong of me and I've apologised. What more do you want?'

He threw her an ambiguous smile. 'I'm coming to that.'

HIGHLAND TURMOIL

BY

STEPHANIE HOWARD

MILLS & BOON LIMITED
ETON HOUSE   18-24 PARADISE ROAD
RICHMOND   SURREY   TW9 1SR

First published in Great Britain 1988
by Mills & Boon Limited

© Stephanie Howard 1988

Australian copyright 1988
Philippine copyright 1988
This edition 1988

ISBN 0 263 76111 8

Set in Palacio 10 on 11½ pt.
01 – 8810 – 52036

Typeset in Great Britain by JCL Graphics, Bristol

Made and printed in Great Britain

CHAPTER ONE

MARCH had come, but winter wasn't over yet. As Sarah came down the castle road, she pulled the green tam-o'-shanter over her ears and raised her eyes to the gathering sky. It would snow soon, she decided with a sigh.

But the weather wasn't really what was on her mind as she came to a halt outside the rusty old castle gates and gazed down the potholed gravel driveway that curved off between the trees. Less than twenty minutes' walk away were home, a hot drink and a roaring fire. And Uncle Dougal, she knew, would be waiting for her. Yet suddenly she was reluctant to go straight back. In spite of her numb cheeks and frozen toes, her curiosity was drawing her towards what lay beyond those rusty iron gates, at the end of the narrow, twisting drive.

'Come on, Glen. Let's take a look.'

The old Shetland collie at her heels glanced up affectionately at his young mistress and wagged his tail, thoroughly approving of this unexpected extension to their regular Sunday afternoon walk. He kept close to the long be-jeaned and booted legs as the big gates swung open with a faintly protesting, creaky sigh and, with a bold toss of her head, Sarah stepped swiftly inside. Trespassing wasn't among her more usual pursuits, but in this case she felt it was justified.

She walked quickly, ignoring the flare of nervous anticipation in her breast, and stuffed her fists into the pockets of her banana yellow anorak. There was nothing to worry about, she told herself. The castle was empty and there wasn't a soul around for miles. And besides, she had to see for herself if what she had heard was true.

She came round the final bend and stopped, feeling her heart leap to her throat as the turreted old greystone building sprang dramatically into view. Only, for once, it wasn't just the beauty of the place that made her gasp—for proud Strathbiggin Castle, once the ancestral home of one of Scotland's most ancient clans, stood encased now from head to toe in newly erected scaffolding.

She frowned. So, it was true. The devil's work had already begun.

Scowling with disapproval, Sarah strode to the big bay windows and peered inside, catching a whiff of fresh plaster and paint. But the light was bad and she couldn't see much. Perhaps it would be better round the back. Alas, there the story was much the same, though she noted with dismay that some of the rear rooms had been partially furnished and there were curtains hanging in place.

And she cursed to think that, soon, some meddling foreigner would be moving in. Then the real destruction would begin!

With a sigh, she turned to gaze out over the acres of glorious heatherclad hill and moor that stretched down to Loch Coih and off as far as the eye could see, and she felt her heart contract with pain. This land that had lain undisturbed for centuries was about to be bulldozed and torn up, to be turned into some ghastly, New-World-inspired, money-catching tourist trap. Strathbiggin would never be the same again. No wonder it made her want to weep.

Disgusted, she turned away. 'I'm getting out of here!'

And it would have been better for her if she had. But, just then, something caught her eye and she was tempted to investigate.

It was tucked away, half out of sight, behind a clump of trees. A large, new-looking Portakabin of the type that builders use. And she felt a sharp stab of resentment as she peered through the window and saw how thoroughly it was kitted out. He was certainly well prepared, this presumptuous new Canadian landowner, Brett McCabe as he was called. Work on the site wasn't scheduled to start until the beginning of next month, when McCabe himself was due to descend, with accompanying fanfare, on the place. Clearly he was a man who believed in leaving nothing to chance.

A strange sort of tapping sound made her glance up. It was one of the cabin windows, she saw at once. The catch had come loose and the metal frame was rattling in the wind. And she smiled to herself as an irresistible idea occurred to her. It would be so easy. All she would have to do was climb up on the pile of planks that were conveniently stacked nearby, fiddle a bit with the half-open catch and she could climb inside. It seemed like an opportunity too good to miss.

'Over there, boy! Lie down!' she commanded the dog. And less than a minute later, her heart beating excitedly, she was clambering over the narrow window-ledge into the shadowy room beyond.

She jumped down and pulled the window closed, then bent to retrieve her green wool hat and stuffed it in her pocket, shaking back her bright auburn hair as she glanced with interest round the room.

Quite clearly, it was the site office. All the equipment told her that. And there, pinned across one entire wall, was a detailed copy of the hateful plans, with, printed in large letters right across the top of it: 'Strathbiggin Sports & Leisure Complex'. Deliberately, she clenched her fists and resisted the urge to tear it down.

The cabin consisted of two main rooms divided by a narrow corridor, at one end of which was the outside door. Sarah decided to examine the room she had entered first, though she had no idea what she was looking for. Still, there must be *something*, she told herself as she rifled assiduously through cupboards and drawers, *some* piece of information tucked away that she could use against McCabe. Maybe even something big enough to stop his scheme from going ahead.

If there was, she never found it. Instead, she was stopped dead in her tracks at the sound of footsteps approaching the outside door. 'Oh, lord!' she muttered to herself. 'Who the devil can that be?'

Whoever it was was not an intruder like herself. A moment later, she heard a key grate in the lock, then heavy male footsteps sounded in the narrow passageway, just a few short feet away on the other side of the partition wall. In alarm, she dropped the file she'd been studying back into its drawer and darted across the room to wedge herself behind the half-open door, nails digging anxiously into her palms, praying that he wouldn't come walking in on her. And it seemed like an agonised eternity till her

prayers were finally answered and she heard the
footsteps disappear into the room across the
passageway.

She should have taken her opportunity to make a
dash for it then, of course, but that stubborn streak of
curiosity in her was too strong to deny. Holding her
breath and infinitely careful not to make a sound, she
tiptoed forward and peered round the door.

He was standing with his back to her, unloading
what appeared to be a box of groceries on to a shelf. A
tall, broad-shouldered figure in a burgundy sweater
and narrow jeans. Youngish—early thirties at a
guess—with a head of short dark hair that appeared
almost black against the fading light. And something
inside her tightened uneasily at the sight of him. For,
though she had never set eyes on him before, she
knew exactly who he was. It was him. The Canadian.
Brett McCabe. All her instincts were telling her so.

Suddenly trembling, she pulled back again and
jammed the green tam-o'-shanter on her head.
Whatever else, he mustn't catch her here. That would
be a calamity. But even as she belatedly prepared to
make a frantic dash for it, she heard the footsteps
turn around and start to come towards her across the
hall. For an instant she froze as panic clawed at her
insides, then in desperation she glanced round,
caught sight of the heavy-based writing-lamp that
was standing on a nearby shelf and, without even
thinking what she was doing, instantly grabbed hold
of it. Automatically she raised it above her head and
held her breath as the door slowly opened and he
stepped inside.

The next few seconds were a blur. There was a

grunt and a dull thud as the lamp made contact before clattering noisily to the floor. Then a strong arm was reaching out, dangerously close to grabbing hold of her. But already she was catapulting across the room, fear lending her unaccustomed speed and strength as she snatched open the window and vaulted outside.

A low, soft whistle summoned Glen, then she was galloping at full stretch back towards the castle, down the potholed driveway and out through the gates. Breathless, and desperately thankful for her lucky escape.

For at that stage she still had no idea of the fatal piece of evidence she had left behind.

'Just take a look at that! Twenty-five more signatures!' Sarah plonked herself down on the edge of Tom's desk and waved the document for him to see. 'Not bad for a weekend's work, I'd say.'

'Not bad at all.' The grey-haired man threw a cautious smile at the slim, vital figure in the blue plaid dress. 'What does that make the total now?'

Sarah made a face. 'Not nearly enough.' She glanced down with a faintly discouraged sigh at the petition in her hand. 'Too few people are prepared to make a stand, and the rest seem convinced that this abominable new leisure centre will be the best thing that's happened to Strathbiggin since the invention of the wheel.'

'And they're probably right.' The quiet-spoken sports editor of the *Strathbiggin Gazette* leaned back a little in his chair and threw his young colleague a tolerant smile. He'd been behind the scheme right from the start and made no secret of the fact. Though he knew his views were wasted on Sarah as he told her for the umpteenth time, 'It's exactly what this town needs. It'll bring money and jobs and prosperity to an area that's been sliding towards poverty and depression for decades now. It's a chance in a million, Sarah. We can't afford to pass it up.'

Sarah sniffed and straightened, tossing back her short auburn hair. 'That's not the way I see it, I'm afraid. I think we're making a big mistake allowing some stranger to move in and start messing up the place.' She frowned a challenge across at Tom. 'Do you really want hordes of tourists descending on the town? All those wretched skiers and climbers and pony-trekkers cluttering up the place? And what about those dreadful buildings he's planning to put up—the skating rink, the bowling alley, the heated swimming pool?' She wrinkled her nose. 'If I had my way, I'd send them swimming in the loch. Then they could all freeze to death.'

Tom laughed. This was one of the few subjects they were destined never to agree upon, but at least they never fell out about it. 'What makes you think it's going to be so dreadful, anyway?' he wanted to know.

'What makes you think it isn't?' Sarah leaned forward earnestly and narrowed her eyes at him. 'Why should we trust McCabe? What does he care about Strathbiggin, after all?'

Tom frowned and ran a hand over his greying hair. 'I can't answer that, I'm afraid. But any man who's prepared to buy up Strathbiggin Castle that's been standing empty and idle for years, along with all the thousands of acres of its estate, and turn the whole lot into something profitable has to have my full support.'

'Well, he doesn't have mine. And there are plenty of others who think like me.' She crossed her long, slim legs and held up a silencing hand beforeTom could utter a word. 'I know what you're going to say—that he's already built a dozen similar centres all over Canada, that he knows what he's doing, that he's a brilliant businessman. But Strathbiggin isn't Ontario, Tom. What works over there isn't necessarily going to fit in here.' She paused for breath. 'Besides, I'll tell you what his motives are. He's already made a huge personal fortune from these projects of his and, quite simply, he wants to add to it. It's not Strathbiggin he cares about. It's a simple matter of dollars and cents.'

Tom threw her a canny look. 'Of course,' he acknowledged with a shrug. 'You couldn't expect the man to pour money into such a scheme if it was going to make him a personal loss. Let's be practical. Making a profit's what it's all about.'

'Precisely! A profit for him!' Instantly, Sarah pounced on him. 'Perhaps you're forgetting that Strathbiggin already has a history of this sort of thing. Systematic exploitation by local landowners is nothing new around these parts. Isn't it precisely the reason why we're in the sorry state we're in today?'

Tom nodded and sighed. 'You're talking about the Baxters, and you're right, of course. I doubt if anyone would disagree.' Then he narrowed his eyes curiously at her. 'But what has the record of

Strathbiggin's foremost family got to do with McCabe?'

'Everything, Tom. He'll exploit the town and its people exactly as the Baxters have always done. All we're doing is exchanging one old master for a newer one.' She frowned and stabbed at the petition with her forefinger. 'That's why I intend to stop him before it's too late.'

'Sarah, the boss wants to see you right away.' Kevin, the junior sub, was at her elbow, beckoning urgently.

Sarah pulled a face at Tom. 'Duty calls,' she smiled. And slid down from the edge of the desk and straightened the skirt of her dress. 'You can save your side of the argument for another time.' Then she stopped off at her own desk to grab a notebook and pen before hurrying through to McAndrew's office at the far end of the reporters' room. When the editor of the *Strathbiggin Gazette* said right away, right away was what he meant!

He was bent over a pile of papers when she walked in, a wiry little man with not much hair and a pair of steel-rimmed spectacles perched precariously on the end of his nose. 'Sit down,' he told her, glancing up. 'I've got a little job for you.'

Sarah sat down expectantly, notebook open, pen eagerly poised. 'A little job' was the description McAndrew invariably reserved for the most important ones.

He pushed a pile of papers aside and regarded her drily over the top of his spectacles. 'There's been a development,' he said. 'Brett McCabe's arrived.'

Sarah shifted uncomfortably in her chair. She

already knew that all too well. Not only had the man arrived, he was probably lying somewhere nursing a fractured skull! And she felt a tingle of anxiety remembering yesterday's shameful events. Not that she believed for one moment that McCabe could be seriously hurt. She hadn't hit him nearly hard enough for that. But, all the same, if McAndrew found out, he'd have her guts for garters—and probably her job as well.

Carefully, she feigned surprise. 'I thought he wasn't due here for a few more weeks.'

'That's what we all thought. I'm afraid he's caught us on the hop.' He frowned, not liking this development at all. 'However, now that he's here, I want you down at the castle right away to do an interview with him. Find out his immediate plans and when he expects the work to start.'

Sarah felt her stomach sink. 'Me, Mr McAndrew? I thought one of the other reporters was to be assigned this job.' Then she added quickly, in support of her case, 'I'm not the best person you could choose. After all, I'm not exactly sympathetic to this scheme of his.' McAndrew was well aware of her anti-McCabe crusade—which he'd insisted she conduct strictly out of office hours.

He gave her a long look now before crisply informing her, 'Precisely why I've decided to assign you to the job. Objectivity and detachment are two important qualities that every journalist must learn. This, Sarah, is your opportunity.'

'But——' she opened her mouth to protest again, but McAndrew cut in.

'What's the matter?' he wanted to know. 'Don't

you think you're up to it?'

That brought her up short. 'It's not that at all.' This would undoubtedly be the biggest assignment she'd ever had, but she had no reservations at all about her ability to handle it. 'It's just that——'

'What?' He cast her a shrewd look that told her it was pointless to go on arguing. 'If there's some problem, you'd better explain.'

She shrugged, defeated. 'No problem,' she said.

'Good.' With an abrupt nod, he turned his attention back to the pile of papers he'd been studying before. 'Have a story on my desk by five o'clock tonight.'

Damn, damn, damn! This was the worst bit of luck she could possibly have had. How could she face McCabe after what had happened yesterday? Still, she consoled herself as she climbed into her beat-up old red Fiat, it had been growing dark at the time of her unfortunate encounter with him, and she doubted very much that he had seen her face. And, thank heavens, her most startling feature, her bright auburn hair, had been totally hidden under her hat!

What was more, today she was dressed quite differently—in a calf-length plaid dress and sheepskin coat—so the chances of him recognising her were really quite remote. And, even if he thought he did, she decided as she set off, she would simply deny everything and tell him he was wrong. Who would ever believe such a story of a reputable *Gazette* journalist?

She decided to leave her car at the castle gates and walk up the driveway under her own steam. The little Fiat's suspension was already quite delicate enough without subjecting it to all these pot-holes. And she stuffed her fists deep into the pockets of her sheepskin coat, feeling the east wind bite at her legs even through the thickness of her woollen tights as she glanced up quickly at the ominous sky. The snow she had predicted yesterday had held off so far. But it was on its way.

There were no signs of life at the front of the castle. He'd be at the site office, round the back—if he was here at all. For it was always possible he'd gone out. Or, even better still, she considered with a hopeful smile, put himself on a plane and flown straight back to Canada.

But no such luck. The first thing she saw as she came round the back was a large blue Range Rover—and an involuntary bell rang in her head. She had seen it before. Yesterday afternoon, from the corner of her eye, as she made her ignominious getaway. She sighed resignedly. So he was here. There was no getting out of this wretched interview after all, it seemed.

The man was partially obscured by the car, and Sarah didn't notice him till she was half-way to the cabin, just a matter of yards away. He was bent over the pile of planks that had served her so conveniently the day before, apparently engrossed in making out some measurements. Sarah's eyes narrowed as she approached. He seemed stockier than he had yesterday, the shoulders beneath the plaid jacket not quite so broad, and the hair that had appeared as black as jet, now, in the light of day, was a much softer brown. Yet one thing about him hadn't changed. He seemed as totally unaware of her eyes on him now as he had been yesterday. Zero out of ten for vigilance, she decided with a superior smile, and deliberately cleared her throat.

The man turned round to look at her then, and an odd sense of disappointment gripped her as she looked into his ruddy, weather-beaten face. She forced a smile. 'Good morning, Mr McCabe,' she said.

'You're looking for me?'

Before the man could open his mouth, a deep voice sounded at her back and she swung round, startled, to find a tall, lean figure standing in the doorway of the cabin, watching her. His arms were folded across his chest, somehow stressing the breadth of the muscular shoulders beneath the leather jerkin he wore. And the hair that sprang back from his strong, tanned brow, she could not but help notice, was almost black. So it had not just been a trick of the light.

She also noticed with some relief that at least he carried no outward signs of yesterday's assault. She straightened. 'I'm looking for you, if your name's McCabe.' Though she knew that already beyond a shred of doubt. Just as she'd known yesterday.

He didn't move. 'Then you're in the right place.' He continued to regard her through a pair of eyes as deeply blue as a mountain lake. 'And you're Miss Sarah Drummond, I presume?'

She stiffened, completely thrown. 'How do you know my name?'

Beneath the tan leather jerkin, he wore a grey wool sweater and slim-cut jeans that hugged the lean, hard hips and softly moulded the muscular thighs. And

there was something positively condescending about
the way he was standing in the doorway observing
her, one broad shoulder leaning against the frame,
boot-clad ankles casually crossed. 'It's a policy of
mine to familiarise myself with the identity of my
visitors,' he informed her in a soft, sarcastic drawl.
'You're an employee of the *Strathbiggin Gazette*.
One of their more junior reporters,' he added
dismissively.

Sarah eyed him with antipathy, though she felt a
sharp sense of relief. McAndrew must have been in
touch. There was no other way he could know so
much. She made no attempt at politeness as she
replied, 'Since you appear to be so well informed,
you're no doubt aware of the reasons why I'm here.'

He threw her a contemptuous smile. 'That's easy.
You're a journalist, aren't you? People of your
persuasion, in my experience, are only ever after one
thing—a story. Any miserable little story they can get
their grubby fingers on.'

Antipathy turned to real dislike. So, apart from all
his other faults, he was one of those people who had
a down on journalists. Suddenly sorry, after all, that
she hadn't done a better job with the lamp, she
forced herself to answer with commendable restraint,
'I'm here to do a job, Mr McCabe. Whether you
happen to like it or not, the people of Strathbiggin
have a right to be kept informed of what you're up to
here. And it's the duty of the *Gazette* to make sure
they are.' McAndrew would be proud of her, she
thought, as she added with dignity, 'That, Mr
McCabe, is why I'm here.'

'Admirable. Devotion to duty is a most

'commendable quality.' For what should have been a compliment, he made it sound remarkably like a slur.

Sarah decided to let it pass. The man was insufferable, but she wasn't here to bandy words with him. 'In that case, you won't object if I ask you a couple of questions?' she said.

'Ask away.' He paused and let his arms drop to his sides. 'I may even see fit to answer one or two of them.' Then he smiled a slow, superior smile. 'But, first, I must insist, there's something you should see.'

Sarah frowned, not trusting him an inch, and narrowed her hazel eyes suspiciously. 'And what might that be?' she wanted to know.

He raised a dark eyebrow at her. 'Something, I feel sure, that will interest you. I confess I found it most enlightening.'

She threw him a bored look. 'Oh, really?' she replied, severely doubting that she would feel the same. She and this man were unlikely to see eye to eye on anything.

'Yes, really.' The blue eyes held hers, all traces of a smile now gone, instead an icy hardness shining in their depths. Then, 'Let's not waste any more time,' he commanded, stepping forward suddenly. 'Kindly follow me.'

She stepped back abruptly, away from him, and stumbled awkwardly. 'Follow you where?' she demanded, an edge to her voice. He had done that deliberately.

'To the house.' And there was cynical amusement in his eyes as he added, 'Ken can accompany us if you feel you need a bodyguard.' He nodded in the

direction of the stocky, red-faced man who had long
since returned to his measuring. 'I'm sure he'd be
only too happy to oblige.'

'Thank you. That won't be necessary.' Sarah's tone
was clipped. He was trying to make her look silly
now, and she resented that.

'Whatever you say.' He stepped past her quickly.
'Ken's my site manager, by the way. He'll be in
charge of the day-to-day running of the project once
the building gets under way.'

'I'll remember that,' she responded acidly, falling
in behind him as he strode off towards the castle—or
the 'house', as he'd so casually referred to it. Perhaps
in the future she could deal with Ken and avoid
further direct contact with McCabe. That might help
to make her job a little less unpalatable.

He walked with long strides, forcing her almost to
scurry to keep up with him. An unsubtle tactic, she
decided, eyeing his broad back resentfully, designed
to underline his supposed male superiority. Brett
McCabe was undoubtedly the sort of man who
expected his women to trot along at six respectful
paces behind him all the time.

He led her up the flight of narrow stone steps to the
rear entrance, then stood aside to let her pass ahead
of him into the wide, high-ceilinged hall. Sarah
glanced round quickly, noting the freshly painted
woodwork and walls, and the quarry-tiled floor, once
chipped and neglected-looking, now beautifully
restored, and grudgingly acknowledged that he'd
done a good job. Then she automatically turned left
towards what she remembered from her childhood
visits as one of the castle's minor reception rooms.

'That's my bedroom you're headed for, Miss Drummond.'

Her hand froze instantly on the door-handle as she swung round stiffly to encounter his amused blue gaze.

'Let's not get ahead of ourselves,' he murmured as her cheeks flared crimson in sudden, fierce embarrassment. 'What I want to show you is in my office over here.'

Sarah glared at him, resenting the mockery in his tone. 'My mistake,' she acknowledged tightly. Heaven forbid that he should even half imagine that it had been deliberate! And, prickling with indignation, she followed him across the hall.

It was a big, stately room with tall casement windows and, at one end, an enormous fireplace where a log fire burned. Much more suited to the grand old dining-hall it had once been than to the crisply functional, high-tech office it had now become.

'Just temporary,' he assured her as she cast a critical eye around. 'I intend building a small extension out back to house the admin offices eventually. But, for the time being, this is my base.'

'Couldn't you have used the site office? Surely it's big enough for two to share?' It was really none of her business, of course, but she was still smarting from his recent provocative remark.

'Not so. Both rooms down there are already spoken for. One is Ken's office, the other is where he'll sleep.'

She might have known. 'Banished to the servants' quarters, I see.' Then she added, her voice heavy with irony. 'Naturally, you couldn't have found a room for him here. There are only about fifty standing empty, I suppose.'

'Sixty-three, to be precise.' There was a warning in his voice, like a parent addressing an impertinent child. 'But, since it seems to concern you so much, the arrangements reflect Ken's preference, not mine.'

'Even better.' She met his cold gaze unrepentantly. 'So much more convenient when the hired help knows its place.'

They were standing in the middle of the room, confronting one another like a couple of bad-tempered dogs. McCabe was the first to make a move. He straightened abruptly and glanced down at her, a scowl of irritation darkening his face. 'Let's just cut the conversation,' he rapped. 'I'd prefer this meeting to be as brief as possible.'

'Likewise, I promise you. You brought me here to show me something. Perhaps you could get on with it.'

'Don't worry, I'll get on with it. Just as soon as you take a seat.'

There was a leatherback chair immediately behind her, she could see it from the corner of her eye. But she remained defiantly upright, glaring at him. 'I can see just as well standing up,' she informed him cuttingly.

For just a fraction of a second, his eyes locked menacingly with hers. Then his hands were on her shoulders and, with the speed of a rocket, her bottom hit the chair. 'I said take a seat!'

It happened so fast, it took Sarah totally by surprise. 'How dare you lay your hands on me?' she spluttered indignantly. And belatedly struggled to free herself from his iron grip.

But the vice-like fingers continued to hold her for a moment more, seeming to dig right through the thickness of the sheepskin and into her flesh. The expression on his face was unrelenting as he warned, 'Then do as you're told, Miss Drummond, and kindly don't waste my time!'

The nerve! 'Who the hell do you think you're talking to? Don't try to tell me what to do!' And she jerked furiously away from him as he released her at last—though she wisely managed to resist the impulse to jump back to her feet again.

'I think it's better that you see what I have to show you sitting down,' he informed her calmly, then turned to the video unit and TV screen at his back and touched a couple of buttons with his fingertips. He lifted down a cassette from a nearby shelf and slotted it into place. 'Besides,' he added sarcastically, 'I'd hate you to miss any of this.'

Sarah glowered mutinously up at him. Her shoulders were still tingling from the recent pressure of his hands, and angry adrenalin was seething through her veins. 'I hope you're not about to subject me to another of those boring promotional films we all had to sit through last year when the plans for this benighted scheme of yours were under review,' she commented scathingly. They might have won over the city fathers and most of the local citizenry, but they hadn't convinced her at all. And he was wasting his time if he thought he could impress her with another one. 'I'm totally immune to your propaganda,' she informed him now.

'Don't worry, Miss Drummond, it's not propaganda you're about to see.' There was a hard glint in his eyes as he picked up the remote control and the screen before her flickered to instant life. 'And I promise you won't be bored.'

She tossed him a look of total disdain. 'Let me be the judge of that.'

But the words died on her lips and her heart froze with horror inside her breast as she recognised the image coming into focus on the screen.

CHAPTER TWO

IT WAS all there, from the moment of her shameful entrance through the Portakabin window to her hasty, undignified exit back out of it again. In stunned, speechless horror, Sarah sat staring at the screen, reflecting as she watched herself rummage through cupboards and drawers that McCabe hadn't been joking about one thing, at least. There was nothing boring about this tape. Excruciating would be a better epithet. And she squirmed in her seat and wished the floor would open up and swallow her. To think it had never even crossed her mind that there might be a camera hidden in the room!

'Fascinating, don't you think?' As the fifteen-minute ordeal came to an end, he flicked the remote control in his hand. 'Are there any bits you'd like me to run over again? The bit at the end with the lamp, perhaps?'

Sadistic swine. She stared down miserably at the floor, not daring to look him in the eye. 'No, thank you,' she said. Once had already been more than enough.

'Now you know how I knew who you were.' He'd remained standing, half leaning against the wall unit where the video and TV screen were housed, appearing to enjoy the spectacle of her humiliation even more than the film itself. 'It took me less than twenty minutes to identify you on the strength of that.'

Sarah paled and snapped round to look at him. 'You didn't show it to anyone, did you?'

He deliberately took his time to answer that, and the blue eyes were as hard as sapphires as they coldly raked her face. 'That wasn't necessary,' he said at last. 'A couple of phone calls were all it took.'

Thank God for that! She breathed with relief as the blood flowed once more through her veins. Impossible as it seemed, the situation might have been worse.

McCabe was still standing there, like a dark, threatening presence, watching her. 'You're just lucky you did nothing more than surprise me with the lamp. It barely grazed my shoulder, you'll be pleased to hear.'

She smiled a weak smile. 'You scared me. It was self-defence. I'd no idea who you were.'

'Liar. I think you did.' He folded his arms across his chest. 'The truth is, you were scared of being caught.' He paused and forced her to lower her eyes. 'Perhaps you wouldn't mind explaining exactly what you were looking for?'

She couldn't explain. She didn't even know herself. And to admit she'd simply been hoping to turn up some piece of information she could use against him was hardly likely to enhance her case. 'I wasn't trying to steal anything,' she assured him worriedly. 'I'm not a thief, if that's what you think.'

'There wasn't anything worth while to steal.' His tone was unforgiving, hard. 'If there had been, I wouldn't have taken so long about walking in on you. I'd have come in and nailed you straight away.'

Sarah's mouth fell open. 'What do you mean?'

'I mean, my dear Miss Drummond, that I knew all along that you were there.' He straightened and smiled a humourless smile. 'You see, I had the pleasure of watching the first part of the transmission live. From this very room.' He nodded towards the row of security monitors by the door. 'Unhappily for you, the site office, and strategic parts of the castle, are under twenty-four-hour surveillance by a network of concealed cameras.' Then he paused before adding sarcastically, 'For your future reference, it might also interest you to know that a highly efficient alarm system is due to be connected later this week.'

It was on the tip of Sarah's tongue to suggest he suffered from an overly suspicious mind. This was Strathbiggin, after all, not the lawless metropolis that he was evidently accustomed to. But she managed to stop herself in time. Right now, such an observation might seem a little out of place.

He continued, 'I'd just got back from picking up some groceries in town and came through here for a routine check. And what did I see on the monitor? A redhead in a yellow anorak turning out the site office drawers.' He paused to scrutinise her ashen face. 'And you still haven't told me what you were after,' he ground.

Sarah shifted uncomfortably. 'Nothing, really,' she lied. 'I just wanted a closer look at the plans.'

'Don't expect me to believe that.' He gestured impatiently. 'The plans are on public display down at the town hall. You're free to study them at any time.'

Lies and evasion were getting her nowhere. He was far too astute and well informed. There seemed to be just one tactic left. She would throw herself on his mercy instead. She smiled a bleak, repentant smile. 'Look, Mr McCabe, I'm sorry for what I did. It was wrong of me and I apologise. But there's no real harm done, after all. Can't we just forgive and forget?'

'Forgive and forget?' A smile curled slowly round his lips, deflating Sarah's slender hopes. 'I'm afraid, Miss Drummond, that isn't really what I had in mind.' He thrust his hands into the pockets of his jeans. 'I know all about you, you see.'

'Oh?' Reluctantly, she met his eyes, wondering what was coming next.

'I know that you don't want me here and that you don't approve of my scheme. You've even started up a petition, I'm told, to try and have it stopped.'

She couldn't deny it. 'It's a free country,' she said.

'And you're wasting your time!' His eyes were hard. 'The project will go ahead whether it has your blessing or not.'

'We'll see.' He was so damned sure of himself. 'The best-laid plans——'

'*Schemes*, not plans,' he corrected her. So he knew his Burns. 'And this one isn't going to "gang a-gley".' He turned and crossed over to the fireplace and stood for a moment with his back to her. 'However, that's not the point. You're entitled to your opinions, as you say.' Then he swivelled round abruptly to look at her. 'What you're not entitled to do is break into my property in order to grub around for some filthy damned story to put in that rag of yours!'

So that was what he thought! 'But you're wrong, Mr McCabe. What I did yesterday had nothing at all to do with my job. I wasn't looking for a story—I swear! It was just personal curiosity.'

He seemed doubtful. 'You mean you weren't on some errand for the *Gazette*?'

'Most definitely not!' If only he knew, it was an outrageous thought! 'What I did had nothing to do with the paper at all. That's not the way the *Gazette* operates.'

He turned away derisively and picked up a huge brass poker from the hearth, then seemed to study it for a moment, weighing it in his hand. Sarah watched, resisting the urge to press her point. Already, she had learned he was not a man to be pressed. He would make up his own mind, in his own good time. There was nothing she could do or say that would influence him.

But there was a question that had been bothering her. She shook her hair back from her face. 'If you knew I was there in the office from the start, why didn't you confront me immediately?'

'I was in no hurry.' As he turned, a callous look flitted across his face. 'And I was curious to see how you'd react. That's why I went through to the other room first—to give you a chance to figure your own way out of the mess.'

'How sporting!' She spat the words at him. It was humiliating to learn that while she'd been sweating in the next room, terrified lest she gave her presence away, he'd been perfectly aware that she was there. 'Playing sadistic little games, I suppose, is how you get your kicks.'

He tapped one of the burning logs with the poker and answered without looking at her. 'Don't try to change the subject, Miss Drummond. I'm not the one whose personal habits are under scrutiny.'

As he leaned over the fireplace, he seemed both composed and threatening at the same time, the poker in his hand an instrument of idle torture as he prodded it among the flames. She licked her lips uneasily as another thought occurred to her. 'Why did you let me get away? You could easily have come after me.' And almost certainly have caught her, too. Against that strong, athletic frame, she wouldn't have stood a chance. 'You could have grabbed me before I even got out of the window if you'd really wanted to.'

He straightened deliberately and let his eyes trail over her, and his tone was mockingly suggestive as he spoke. 'Is that what you wanted me to do?' he asked.

'Of course not!' Sarah flushed indignantly. 'My only desire was to escape.' She paused and narrowed her eyes at him. 'But you must have had your reasons for letting me get away.'

'Of course.' He smiled and tossed the poker down in the hearth. 'The reasons are obvious.' And he raised a superior dark eyebrow at her. 'The encounter, remember, was being taped. To apprehend you I would have needed to use force. As much as that might have suited my mood, I risked putting myself in the wrong. Let's just say it suited my long-term purposes much more to leave it quite unequivocal who the real villain was.'

Calculating bastard! 'You're so damned smart.'

'I'd say I need to be, with unsavoury characters like you around.'

'It takes one to know one, as they say.' She threw him a look of cold contempt. 'No doubt that sort of deviousness comes naturally to you.'

'And your prying nature seems admirably suited to your trade.'

She'd been half expecting that. 'A trade for which, I gather, you have little respect.'

'Not the trade,' he corrected her. 'Just some of the people who practise it.'

'What's the matter? Do you have so many secrets you need to hide?'

'If I do, you'll never uncover them.' He held her eyes. 'I don't leave them lying around in drawers.'

Exposed and suddenly embarrassed, she snatched her gaze away. What an incautious fool she'd made of herself! She'd made an enemy of a man it would have been wiser not to tangle with.

'It's a pity,' McCabe continued now. 'In spite of my reservations, I generally manage to get along with the Press, and I'd been hoping it might prove possible to do likewise here. The reports I'd had about McAndrew suggested he was a man of integrity.'

'He is.'

'Alas, however, not a quality he shares with certain junior members of his staff.'

Sarah took a deep breath. 'I've already told you, what I did had nothing whatsoever to do with my work on the *Gazette*. And I've admitted it was wrong of me and I've apologised. What more do you want?'

He threw her an ambiguous smile. 'I'm coming to that.' Then he bent to toss a log on the fire, scattering a spray of white-hot sparks. Yet an ominous chill hung in the air as he straightened suddenly and crossed to one of the windows, then stood for a moment with his back to her, silently looking out. The pale, wintry light cast a blue sheen over the jet-black hair and sharpened the strong, straight lines of his face. At last he said, 'Since it seems I have no choice but to have dealings with this paper of yours, there's one small stipulation I'd like to make.'

So he was going to try and dictate terms. She didn't like the sound of that. 'What stipulation?' she enquired.

He turned so that his back was to the light, his features totally obscured. 'I want *you* assigned to this story and no one else.'

'I already have been.' But it seemed an odd request. The opposite would have made more sense. She frowned across at him. 'Why me?' she asked.

He didn't answer right away. Instead, he came back across the room at a leisurely pace, pointedly removed the incriminating tape from the VCR and returned it to the shelf. Then turned to look at her as he observed, 'Let's just say you're one member of the local Press whose co-operation I feel I can rely upon.'

Sarah could scarcely believe her ears. 'Do I detect a whiff of blackmail, Mr McCabe?'

'Nothing so crude.' He feigned distaste. 'I'm merely suggesting an arrangement that could be to our mutual benefit. I don't want some scandal-seeking hack snooping around here, interfering with my workers and generally getting in my hair.' He paused and smiled, a poisonous smile. 'And you don't want to lose your job.'

She gasped, and would have walked out on him

there and then if she hadn't had so much to lose. 'What you're suggesting is highly unethical!' she protested indignantly. 'I won't be a part of it, so you can forget the idea right now. That isn't the way we operate in Strathbiggin, I'm afraid.'

'No, Miss Drummond, I'm aware of that. Such straightforward arrangements are not your style at all.' He paused to shake his head contemptuously at her. 'I'm afraid this sudden high moral tone of yours is totally wasted on me. I have proof, remember, of the ethical code of behaviour to which, in practice, you subscribe.'

'That was a lapse, Mr McCabe. I've never done anything like it before.'

'That fact is immaterial.' With a sigh of impatience, he sat down in one of the deep leather armchairs and frowned across at her. 'If you refuse to co-operate with me, I shall have no hesitation at all in bringing your off-duty activities to the attention of your editor.'

'You wouldn't!'

'You misjudge me, Miss Drummond. I'm afraid I would.'

Sarah stared at him helplessly. Beyond a doubt she knew he would.

He smiled a harsh smile. 'I shall not press charges, though breaking and entering—not to mention assault—are criminal offences, as you know. But I shall insist that he fire you. Right away.'

Her mouth had gone dry. There would be no need for him to insist. If McAndrew as much as caught a glimpse of that tape, she'd be straight out on her ear. Yet, devastating as it would be, losing her job would

be the easiest part. The hard part would be living
with the shame. It would shatter her—and Uncle
Dougal, too. She straightened her shoulders and
confronted McCabe. 'I can't let you do that,' she said.
To cast such disgrace upon her family was quite
unthinkable.

He held her eyes without mercy. 'Then you know
what to do. Co-operate!'

'With *you*?' The idea was repellent, in spite of the
alternative.

He shrugged, indifferent to her fate. 'That's the
deal, I'm afraid.'

A pause. 'And what exactly would this co-
operation involve?' she demanded warily.

'Simple.' He leaned back in his chair and laced his
long, tanned fingers across his chest. 'I shall supply
you with information about what's going on, and
you, in return, will see to it that it's printed as and
when I require.'

'That's out of the question! Quite impossible!'

He deliberately misunderstood and threw her a
cynically reassuring smile. 'Don't worry, I'll make
sure you get all the information you need.
Remember, it's in my interests, too, to get adequate
coverage for the scheme.'

'*Favourable* coverage! That's what you really mean!'

He ignored the sarcasm in her remark. 'And why
should it be otherwise? You seem to be unaware of
the fact, but I'm pouring a great deal of money into
this town. Money it's badly in need of, as far as I can
see.'

'You're breaking my heart! Don't tell me you're
looking for gratitude as well!' She threw him a look of

harsh dislike. 'Am I supposed to consider you some sort of public benefactor? Because I don't, I'm afraid.'

He ran his eyes slowly over her face, his expression quite unfathomable. 'And what *do* you consider me to be, Miss Drummond? Perhaps you'd like to tell me that?'

'My pleasure. Since you ask, I consider you someone this town could do very well without. Another Baxter, to be precise.'

'And what is that supposed to mean?' He raised a curious eyebrow at her.

'The Baxters are your next-door neighbours, Mr McCabe. Well-heeled folk, much like yourself, who've been bleeding Strathbiggin dry for over two hundred years.' Her tone was cutting as she went on, 'They like to pose as benefactors, too. But the only people they've ever benefited are themselves.'

He sat forward in his seat and fixed her with a stony stare. 'Don't try to draw me into your petty local politics. That's not what I'm here for.'

'Oh, I know what you're here for all right . . .'

'I'm here to do a job of work, and that's really all that concerns me right now.'

'Typical! Just the attitude I'd expect!'

In sudden irritation, he rose from his chair. 'Your expectations, Miss Drummond, I assure you, are of absolutely no interest to me.'

'I doubt anything other than your own welfare is.' Just to annoy him, she stood up, too.

They were standing less than a metre apart and, all at once, he felt dangerously close. Even beneath the tan, the pallor of anger shone from his face, and she could feel it radiating from his hard, taut frame like some violent and unpredictable force. But she somehow willed herself to stay her ground, and stared back defiantly at him. If he dared to lay another hand on her, she'd simply scream the damned place down!

But the hard lines around his eyes and mouth softened unexpectedly as he shoved his fists into the pockets of his leather jerkin and smiled at her sardonically. 'You have quite an impressive line in moral outrage, Miss Drummond—for one whose record in such matters is not exactly squeaky clean.'

Suddenly deflated, she looked away. In the heat of the moment, she'd forgotten that.

His eyes bored into the top of her head. 'So, to return to the matter in hand, have you decided yet?'

'Decided what?' She was playing for time.

'I'm waiting for an answer.' His tone was sharp. 'Can I rely on your co-operation or not?'

Reluctantly, she cleared her throat. 'Within reason. Possibly.'

'I'm afraid that's not good enough. Do you agree or don't you? I want to know.'

Sarah scowled down at the floor. 'What alternative do I have?'

'None.' He spoke the word with triumph. 'So, it's a deal?' And, with an irritating smile, he withdrew one hand from his jerkin pocket and held it out to her. 'Let's shake on it, shall we?'

Her own hands were stuffed into the pockets of her coat and she would gladly have kept them there. Forcing her to shake hands with him was simply rubbing salt into the wound. She threw him a disdainful look. 'Shaking hands is for gentlemen. I don't see any here.'

But he continued to stand there with his hand outstretched, a powerful, unsettling presence that somehow filled her with unease. And she cursed herself for the foolish lapse that had left her so vulnerable to him. For he had her hamstrung. They both knew that.

'Come along, Miss Drummond. What are you waiting for?'

With a show of reluctance, she dragged her hand from her pocket and held it out to him. 'I want you to know it goes against all my principles to agree to this.'

'I doubt very much that that fact will cause you to lose sleep. As we've already seen, your principles, Miss Drummond, are quite conveniently disposable.' His grip as he clasped her hand was firm and cool, and the contact between them brief. Yet Sarah almost snatched her hand away, shocked and confused by the unexpected searing impact of his naked flesh on hers.

He seemed not to have noticed the reaction he had stirred in her as he stepped back abruptly and turned away. 'And now, if you don't mind, I've got work to do. I suggest that we wind up our little tête-à-tête.'

Her feelings precisely. 'Please don't neglect your responsibilities on my account,' she advised him with a dry smile.

'Don't worry, Miss Drummond, there's absolutely no danger of that.' He glanced caustically over his shoulder as he led her to the door. 'Fortunately, some of us have our priorities straight.' And he quickly pulled the door open and stood aside to let her pass.

With all the dignity she could muster, Sarah swept past, acutely conscious of his eyes on her, though she kept her own fixed straight ahead. Inside, she was sizzling with rage. McCabe was twice as much of a monster as she'd ever feared, and his arrival on the scene was much more than a simple disaster for the town. It was an outright personal catastrophe for her.

'One more thing——' He closed the door behind them as she started to hurry down the steps. 'I'd like you to stop off at the site office for a minute or two. I've a couple of bits of information already printed out that I'd like you to use in the paper tonight. Then we needn't bother with those questions you were planning to ask.'

Sarah made a face. In her anxiety to escape, she'd quite forgotten why she'd come. 'Of course,' she consented. Then added mockingly, 'A press release, no less. How incredibly organised.'

He ignored the jibe and instantly took the wind out of her sails. 'At some later date,' he informed her with a faintly dictatorial smile, 'I shall require a couple of hours of your time to show you round the site and explain the plans in detail before the work gets under way.'

She cringed at the thought. A couple of hours in the company of Brett McCabe had about as much appeal as a broken leg. But she forced a sarcastic smile. 'My pleasure. And when would be convenient for you?'

They'd reached the Portakabin door. He paused to look down at her. 'Don't worry, Miss Drummond. I'll let you know.'

Arrogant bastard, she fumed. But, just as she was

about to come back at him, Ken appeared. Politely, but briefly, McCabe introduced the two of them. 'Ken, this is Miss Sarah Drummond, our representative of the local Press. No doubt you'll be seeing quite a lot of her.' Then, leaving Sarah to ponder that last remark, he strode indoors, instructing her, 'Wait here, I'll only be a minute or two.'

Ken threw her a friendly smile. 'I take it you're a local girl?'

She smiled back. 'Born and bred,' she replied, and wondered quietly to herself how she could ever have mistaken this man for McCabe. They were roughly the same height and age, but the similarities ended there. Ken was heavier, though not so muscularly built, with none of the electric presence of McCabe, and he had a shy and diffident manner, quite unlike his boss. 'And how about you?' she asked him conversationally. 'Where do you come from?'

He grinned. 'Fife,' he answered with pride. 'I've never spent time in the Highlands before. It's a very beautiful part of the world.'

Sarah nodded. At least, it had been before McCabe came along. What it would be like when he'd finished was another matter entirely. But she could scarcely blame Ken for that. She smiled at him. 'Just wait until the summer. It can be absolutely glorious then.'

'Here we are.' McCabe appeared in the doorway, making her jump, and held out a slim buff folder to her. 'I think this should cover your immediate needs.'

Stiffly, avoiding his eyes, she accepted it.

'And now, if you don't mind, I'll accompany you to your car.'

'There's no need for that. Besides,' she added, suddenly remembering, 'I'm parked outside the gates.'

'Then I'll drive you to the gates.'

Such chivalry. Though he disabused her of that unlikely notion right away.

'You do have such an unfortunate tendency to stray; I feel it would be wise to see you off the premises.'

Irked, she glanced across at Ken, wondering what he'd made of that last remark. But the site manager had already detached himself from them and was gazing out across the fields. Feeling her eyes on him, he turned round apologetically. 'You're leaving, are you? Well, it's been a pleasure meeting you.'

'And you.' She threw him a genuine smile. At least there was one person involved in this detested scheme who possessed a gram of civility.

Unlike McCabe. He was already striding off along the drive, clearly above such humble pleasantries. She hurried to catch up with him, eyeing the long, loping legs with intense dislike as a sudden question occurred to her. She cleared her throat and enquired casually as she came abreast of him, 'How long will you be staying in these parts?'

'Just long enough to see the project on its feet. I'll be handing over the reins to the contractors then.'

He was being deliberately obtuse. Keeping the irritation from her voice, she tried again to pin him down. 'Have you any idea how long that will be?'

'Not exactly, I'm afraid.' He turned to her with a smile, the smile of a big cat unhurriedly rounding up its prey. 'Two or three months was my original estimate, but I may stay on for the summer if I decide I like it here.'

Her heart sank to her boots as she stared down at the potholed drive. In that case, she must try to ensure that he absolutely hated it. She took a deep breath. 'It's a lovely place, of course, but perhaps a bit lonely for a man on his own.' She'd heard he was single, unattached. 'I'm afraid there's very little social life.'

'That's all right by me. I quite enjoy a bit of peace and quiet.'

'And the nearest big town's nearly two hours' drive away.'

'Is that so? But you manage, don't you?'

She shrugged. 'I'm used to it.' Though, at times, even she longed for a bit more excitement in her life. 'Someone like yourself would find it very dull.'

He threw her a half-smile and paused as they reached the gates. 'Don't worry about me, Miss Drummond,' he said. 'I'm sure I'll manage to find something to keep me amused.'

It was just at that moment that a pair of riders appeared at the end of the road, coming towards the castle entrance at a slow, steady pace. McCabe's eyes narrowed curiously, but Sarah had recognised them instantly. 'Damn!' she muttered under her breath. She'd timed her exit very badly indeed.

'Morning.' The heavy-set figure on the leading steed drew up alongside the castle gates and smiled politely at McCabe. Then shifted his gaze for a fraction of a second to the girl with the auburn hair. 'Miss Drummond,' he acknowledged with a brief, curt nod.

With an effort, Sarah responded with the semblance of a smile. 'Mr Baxter,' she replied.

'So you've already been tracked down by the Press.' The slim blonde girl in the immaculate riding gear reined up alongside her father and bestowed a sympathetic smile on Brett McCabe. 'How very tiresome for you.'

As McCabe returned the smile, Sarah wondered bitchily if he had any idea of how privileged he was. It wasn't with everyone that Amanda Baxter and her father stopped to pass the time of day. And a surge of irrational irritation went through her as he reached out to rub the muzzle of Amanda's mount. 'A handsome filly,' he observed, holding the blonde girl's eyes,

'Settling in all right?' old man Baxter wanted to know. 'Don't forget, if you need anything, we're just a phone call away.'

Sarah nearly laughed out loud. This display of neighbourliness was not like Baxter at all. She bit her lip and glanced at McCabe as he replied, 'That's very kind of you. I'll keep your offer in mind.'

'Be sure you do.' Baxter's mount was growing restless. He started to move away. 'In the meantime, we'll expect you round for dinner tomorrow evening, if that's still all right.'

She must be hearing things! Her gaze darted from Baxter back to McCabe, totally entranced by this exchange.

He was leaning casually against the gate-post, a composed smile on his face. And his eyes were fixed on Amanda. 'Perfect,' he replied.

The blonde girl threw him a dazzling smile. 'Shall

we say around eight o'clock?'

'Eight o'clock,' he confirmed with a nod. 'You can count on it. I'll be there.'

'I look forward to it.' She swung round to follow her father. 'We'll see you then.'

As the Baxters trotted off, Sarah threw McCabe a look of disgust. So he'd already made the acquaintance of the local lairds, and evidently had lost no time in declaring allegiance with them. She might have guessed. Irritably, she turned away towards her car, snatched open the driver's door and flung the folder he had given her into the rear seat. All she had suspected about him was true. He was just like them. Perhaps even worse.

'Goodbye, Miss Drummond.' As she clambered in behind the wheel, he was suddenly right there, leaning down to look at her, one hand resting lightly on the open door.

She stared straight ahead and started the engine up. 'Goodbye,' she answered between clenched teeth, and jammed the gearstick into first.

'Drive safely,' he advised, stepping back and slamming the door. 'You'll be hearing from me.'

How nice, Sarah reflected sarcastically, and jammed her foot down on the accelerator. The little red car shot forward with a squeal of protest and a spray of stones—a pointless and puny gesture, as she realised all too well. She was outmanoeuvred and outnumbered. Out of her depth and out of her class. McCabe had strung her up like a puppet and she had no choice but to dance to his tune.

At least, for now.

As she sped off down the road, she cast a challenge

through her rear-view mirror at the tall, dark figure
still standing by the castle gates. And fierce defiance
glittered in her eyes.

'You may have won this battle, Brett McCabe!' she
muttered to herself. 'But the war has just begun!'

CHAPTER THREE

'SO, THIS is the monster you've been telling me about!'

Dougal was in the kitchen having breakfast, a copy of the early edition of the *Gazette* spread out on the table in front of him, when Sarah appeared in the doorway, tousle-haired and still in her bright pink towelling robe. He glanced up and jabbed at the photograph that dominated the front page. 'He doesn't look so bad to me.'

'What did you expect? Two heads?' Sarah smiled and leaned over his shoulder to plant a good-morning kiss, observing with mixed feelings that her story on McCabe had made the front page. 'Appearances can be deceptive,' she assured him, noting with annoyance that the paper's photographer had done an unusually flattering job. He had caught the new local landowner in a sympathetic pose, looking more like a hero than the villain he really was. 'Don't worry,' she promised her uncle with a frown. 'He's every bit as nasty as I said he was.'

Dougal sighed and stroked his beard. 'If you say so, lass,' he agreed. 'There are lines of ruthlessness in that face, all right, but at least I'd say it was an honest one.'

Well, that was wrong for a start! As she crossed to the cooker and helped herself to a plateful of porridge, Sarah smiled a bitter smile. The man was a blackmailer, a bully and an outright rogue, and for once Dougal's judgement had let him down. She glanced at him over her shoulder and shook her head. 'The camera can lie, you know.'

'Aye, I suppose you're right.' He turned his attention to her report. 'Now, let's see what this is all about!'

As she ate, Sarah watched him from the corner of her eye with a mixture of affection and regret. Those grizzled, greybeard features meant everything in the world to her. It was for Dougal's sake, more than her own, that she had agreed to McCabe's demands.

She bit her lip in sudden shame, knowing how badly she'd let him down. Though a humble shepherd all his life, he was a deeply honest and honourable man. He would never be able to understand the foolish thing that she had done. Nor would he be able to live with the shame if the story should ever get out. Though he would stand by her, the disgrace of it would literally cripple him. And she owed him so much better than that. She owed him everything. For the better part of her twenty-four years, he'd been both father and mother to her.

'It's a good report.' He laid down the paper and looked up at her, the shrewd grey eyes, despite their sixty-seven years, still unaided by spectacles. 'An informative, well-balanced piece, if I may say so,' he added with pride.

It took all of her will-power not to drop her eyes. 'Merely an exercise in objectivity and detachment—essential attributes in my line of work.' There was a twist of cynicism in her voice as she parroted her boss's words. The truth was, she had simply paraphrased the pile of notes McCabe had given her—then suffered a pang of acute embarrassment when McAndrew, like Dougal, had praised the result.

But the old man was only half listening. He was bent over her report again. 'It says here he's already recruited over fifty local artisans, and expects to more than double that figure within the next few months.' He clicked his tongue approvingly. 'That can't be bad.'

'It's peanuts when put alongside the damage he's going to do.' Sarah was quick to put him right.'And, anyway, these are only short-term jobs. They won't change anything. I'll bet you won't see any locals actually running things. I've already met his site manager, and he's a Lowlander, for a start.'

Dougal shrugged. 'You can't blame him for that. There aren't many people of that sort of calibre left around these parts.'

That irked her. 'Are you defending him?'

'Not at all.' Dougal glanced across at her irritated face. 'Just being realistic, lass.' He sighed and leaned back in his chair. 'I'm on the same side as you, don't forget. Didn't I sign that petition of yours? I want the best for Strathbiggin, too.'

'Then you don't want McCabe.' She pushed her half-empty plate aside. 'Just look at the man! Barely arrived, and already he's made it perfectly clear which side of the fence he's on. He's with the Baxters—and that should tell you all you need to know. No friend of the Baxters is a friend of this town.'

Dougal Drummond needed no reminding of that. When it came to the Baxters, he bore his own private scars. His brow puckered thoughtfully as he bent to stroke the dog that lay sleeping at his feet. Then he sighed again and shook his head as a long, shaggy tail thumped blissfully. 'It's a pity,' he murmured, almost to himself. 'In spite of everything, I'd rather been hoping he might turn out to be different.'

'Well, he isn't. He's rude, overbearing and out for himself. A carbon copy, if you ask me.' She glanced up quickly at the kitchen clock and started to push back her chair. 'Take my word for it, you wouldn't approve of him, one bit.'

As she began to gather up the dirty plates, Dougal reached out a restraining hand. 'Don't you bother with that,' he told her. 'Mrs Campbell comes today.'

Sarah smiled. 'You and your Mrs Campbell,' she teased, and dropped a kiss on the weather-beaten cheek. 'I've told you a hundred times, you don't need to waste money paying for help.'

'And what should I do instead? Expect you to cook and clean for me when you've got a full-time job as well?'

'I could manage.'

'Well, I won't let you.' His tone was firm and full of pride. 'That's not what I sent you to college for. And besides,' he added reasonably, 'it's only a couple of coppers a week, and it comes in handy for her since her husband died.' He picked up the paper, declining to pursue the argument. 'Now, be off with you, my girl, and earn that handsome salary of yours!'

In her room, as she hurriedly dressed, Sarah reflected with a bitter smile the enormous debt she owed the old man. Since the age of ten, when her mother had died, he'd been the only family she had. And, though a middle-aged widower at the time, with no experience of children of his own, he'd set to to the task of bringing her up with unstinting love and enthusiasm. No sacrifice had been too great, no demand too high. And it had been his greatest pride when she'd landed a job on the *Strathbiggin Gazette*.

She sat down on the edge of the bed and stuffed her feet into high leather boots. And just look how she'd repaid him! By risking the Drummonds' good name in Strathbiggin! She drew in her breath frustratedly and shook her glossy auburn head. All she had ever wished for was just to be worthy of him. To justify his faith and love, and somehow live up to all his dreams. But with one rash and badly calculated move she'd risked shattering that hope for good.

Out in the hallway, she paused to pull on her anorak and stuck her head round the kitchen door. 'I'm off now, Uncle Dougal!' she called.

'OK, lass.' He paused and glanced round thoughtfully. 'I was just wondering if I might have a word with Mrs Campbell today and ask if she wouldn't mind coming round to cook us a special dinner some night.'

Sarah frowned at him. 'What are we celebrating?' she wanted to know.

He didn't answer directly, but asked another question instead. 'When do you think you might be seeing Brett McCabe again?'

An alarm bell sounded in her head. 'I've no idea. Why do you ask?'

He stroked his beard. 'There are certain Highland customs I think we're duty-bound to observe.'

'What customs?' He was up to something.

'Customs of hospitality. He is our neighbour, after all.'

'And our enemy.'

'Perhaps.' He threw her a canny look. 'But you know what they say—keep your friends close, but your enemies closer. I'd like to meet him face to face.' He turned back to the newspaper. 'Next time you see him, lass, invite him round for a meal some night.'

A day later, she had her opportunity. McCabe telephoned her at the office. 'Come round before lunch,' he instructed. 'I want to show you round the site.'

Not so much as a please, she observed with irritation to herself. He obviously expected her to leap eagerly to his command. 'I'll try,' she answered drily, resentment in her voice.

'Don't try. Just be there. I'll expect you at eleven o'clock.'

She arrived at thirteen minutes past. Another puny gesture, she acknowledged as she parked her car at the end of the drive and headed towards the castle on foot. But it was a gesture, at least. Let him not be in any doubt about how unwilling her co-operation was.

It had snowed on and off for the past two days, and a thick, white carpet covered the ground. As she trudged towards the castle, Sarah cursed him under her breath. She could have done extremely well without the chore of coming here today. And she frowned with irritation at the sets of parallel tyre trcks that sliced like tramlines through the virgin snow, then glared as they led to the big blue car that was parked around the back. Why did he have to come into her life?'

'I can see I'm going to have to buy you a watch!'

She was half-way up the rear entrance stairs when the door was flung open and he was standing there. She looked defensively into the grim, hard face. 'It was the snow,' she bluffed. 'I got held up.'

He was dressed in a charcoal sweater and charcoal trousers, and at such uncomfortably close proximity, he seemed to tower over her. 'Then, next time, you'd better make allowances,' he rasped. 'If you're more than five minutes late for an appointment again, I'm afraid our deal is off!' The blue eyes blazed a warning from the dark-tanned face. 'I'm not one of your boyfriends, who's got nothing better to do with his time than hang around and wait for you!'

Perish the thought! As he stepped back to let her pass into the hall, it was on the tip of Sarah's tongue to inform him that she had no current boyfriend to keep hanging around, let alone a string of them, and that she reserved her unpunctuality exclusively for people she disliked. But she bit the comment back and threw him a sarcastic smile. 'I'll do my best to remember that.'

'Make sure you do.' An amused smile flitted across his face. 'It would be a shame to blot your copy-book now after such an auspicious start. That front-page piece you wrote the other day was really quite good.' Then he killed the compliment by brusquely adding, 'I shall continue to expect that standard from you.'

She glowered at him, resenting the way he revelled in the role of ringmaster. She could almost hear the crack of the whip. 'I hope not to disappoint you,' she answered with a twist.

'Make sure you don't.' He raised a coal-black eyebrow at her. 'Just remember, one foot wrong and that tape gets its public première.' He turned and strode into his office across the hall, adding over his shoulder as she followed him through the door. 'By the way, I should point out—just in case you should have any ideas about confiscating the evidence while you're here—that particular tape is no longer here. I now have it under lock and key.'

The cruel allusion stopped her in her tracks. 'I've already told you, I'm not a thief!'

He smiled a dismissive smile. 'Alas, I have only your word for that. I prefer a more substantial guarantee.' He paused. 'But now, before I take you on our little tour, I have something else for you to see.'

He walked briskly ahead of her, to a door at the far end of the room, with long, loose strides, broad shoulders moving sinuously beneath the dark wool sweater he wore. Sarah followed, hating him. He never lost a single opportunity to try and put her down, to remind her of his hold on her and the vulnerable position she was in. But he was wrong if he thought he could make her cringe. Nobody, not even Brett McCabe, was capable of doing that!

'This is it.' He opened the door and led her into a smaller ante-room. 'This should give you a clearer picture of how the centre will look when it's built.'

Sarah's eyes widened as she came to a stop,

reluctantly impressed by what she could see laid out in front of her. Then, cautiously, she stepped forward to take a closer look.

It was a scale model of the plans, quite meticulously done, with the detail on the castle so true that it appeared almost like a hologram. She bent with interest to study the rest: the additional buildings, like offices, stables and an enormous stadium; the various playing fields scattered about; the covered walkways; the ingeniously placed restaurant that overlooked it all. And none of it was quite as she'd expected it would be. She glanced up non-committally. 'Very interesting,' she said.

'As you can see, we've tried to maintain as far as possible the character of the place. The aim was to make the new structures as much like outbuildings as possible. Extensions of the castle. Complementary to it.' He was standing at her shoulder, the blue eyes on her face.

She moved away. 'I see.' And slowly circled the enormous table where the model was set up. Though she hated to admit it, he had succeeded in his aim. In spite of their clean, modern lines, the buildings had been designed in style, all constructed of local stone and with none standing more than two storeys high. And the strategic replanting of shrubbery and trees lent the whole a unified look.

He lifted down a wooden pointer from a rack and leaned across the table now. 'As you already know, the castle is to be converted into a hostel of sorts.' He pushed back the sleeves of his sweater and pointed with his stick. 'This row of buildings here will provide additional beds. We expect to be able to accommodate around three hundred and fifty guests at any one time.'

At last she had something to criticise! Perversely pleased, Sarah detached her gaze from the strong brown arms where it had accidentally strayed, and lifted her eyes to look at his face. 'That should effectively put the local small hotels and boarding houses out of business,' she drily observed.

'Not so, Miss Drummond.' He straightened. 'The guests the centre will be catering for would not have come to Strathbiggin otherwise, so we shall be taking nothing away from the local hoteliers. On the contrary——' he laid down his pointer and folded his arms '—they will undoubtedly benefit from the increase in local activity that the centre generates. Since most of them enjoy less than thirty per cent occupancy, even during the summer months, I imagine they'll welcome the boost to trade.'

So he was back on that bogus philanthropic tack again! She looked him straight in the eye. 'And how much profit do you personally expect to make on the enterprise, Mr McCabe?'

He didn't answer right away, but met her steely gaze with faintly humorous disdain. 'Any profit that accrues will be ploughed straight back into the project to provide additional facilities. However,' he informed her with an acid smile, 'I don't expect any profit at all for the first five years at least.'

She raised a sceptical eyebrow at him. 'I don't believe that,' she said.

'Believe what you will.' He gestured round the ante-room with its newly restored cornices and wood panelling. 'Just to refurbish the castle alone—rewire it, replace the plumbing that's been here since before the ark, put in central heating, repoint the outside and repair the roof—is going to cost many times more than it would cost to build a place of similar size from scratch. Preserving your heritage, Miss Drummond, is a very costly affair.'

She sniffed. 'So why don't you just tear the whole lot down and put up some modern monstrosity in its place? I'm sure that would suit your purposes just as well?'

'Since the castle's a listed building, it would also be against the law—as I'm sure you already know.' Deliberately, he held her eyes. 'Personally, I prefer to stay within the law and leave such acts of criminality to those who have a taste for them.'

He'd done it again! Irked, she drew herself up to her full height. 'I think I've seen enough of this. I'd like to get on with the tour of the site, if you don't mind.'

'Not in the least.' He gestured mock-politely towards the door. 'Later, I'll give you some photographs of the model that I'd like you to use with your article.'

She swept past him into the office. 'Whether or not your pictures are used will depend upon the editor.' Maybe he owned Strathbiggin estate—and even herself, to some extent—but he didn't own the *Gazette* as well!

The door closed behind him with a disinterested click. 'In that case, be sure to make it clear to him that I want them given a fair bit of space.' Then he was striding ahead of her across the office and into the hall. 'Wait here, if you don't mind,' he instructed—

and glanced at her with superior amusement as he crossed to the room on the other side.

Sarah stopped dead and glared at him. It was the room she had almost strayed into by accident the other day and, for once, she had not the slightest inclination to disobey. Yet she followed him discreetly with her eyes, curious in spite of herself.

It was an unashamedly luxurious room. A thick-pile, gold-coloured carpet adorned the floor, and what looked like a cocktail cabinet and fridge were ranged alongside the enormous bed. A fleeting image of him lying between the silky sheets, his bronzed and naked torso propped against a pile of pillows and a glass of some exotic cocktail at his lips, flashed decadently through her head. With a flutter of discomfort, she chased it away. Good God, she was suffering from hallucinations now!

'OK, I'm ready. Let's get started, shall we?'

Before she had time to turn away, he appeared in the bedroom doorway, pulling the zipper of his leather jerkin shut. Suddenly anxious to escape, she flushed and headed for the outside door.

'Allow me.' He was right behind her as she grappled with the knob and struggled for a moment with the weight of the door. Then his arm brushed her shoulder, sending shock-waves to her feet, as he stretched past to assist her with a brief, mocking smile. 'You're more adept with windows, I see!'

Damn him! On wobbly legs, she hurried down the steps and waited impatiently while he locked the door. Would he never let her forget? As he appeared alongside her, she stepped smartly aside. 'Which way now?' she snapped bad-temperedly.

He nodded calmly towards the Range Rover. 'The car's over there,' he said.

'Can't we walk?' Hiking around the snow-clad countryside didn't in itself hold much appeal, but the thought of being cooped up with him in that car was suddenly acutely disquieting.

He frowned. 'We're not going on some leisurely Sunday afternoon stroll, so if it's all the same to you, we'll take the car.' Without bothering to wait for her reply, he crossed to the car and opened the passenger door for her.

Without further protest, she climbed inside. At least it would be quicker by car. The ordeal of his company would be over that much sooner than if they were to go on foot.

She'd forgotten how enormous the estate was, stretching as it did from the outskirts of the town to the barren, brooding slopes of Ben a-Coih.

'Not all of it will be developed, of course. In fact, by far the greater part will remain untouched.' He'd pulled up at a strategic point at the head of the glen with a marvellous view out over the loch. 'But we'll be building special facilities for climbers and hill-walkers—bad weather shelters and the like.' He pointed towards a snow-clad peak. 'Down there's where we'll build the téléférique.'

As Sarah glanced across at him, she felt a sharp rush of antipathy. He was such a total autocrat. So unbearably sure of himself. 'How does it feel,' she enquired scathingly, 'to be tampering with one of the oldest, most historic sites in all the world?' She paused, deliberately baiting him. 'I suppose you must feel a bit like God?'

He turned round very slowly to look at her and the dark blue eyes were as hard as flints. The muscles around his jaw had tightened and the wide, forceful mouth straightened to a thin, hard line. 'Miss Drummond,' he answered unhurriedly, 'land development is my work. It's what I'm good at. It's what I know. It gives me a great deal of satisfaction to take a piece of idle land and make something productive out of it. I get an enormous sense of achievement when it all works out.' He paused and held her eyes for one uneasy moment more. 'But to answer your question—no, it doesn't make me feel like God.'

As the warmth rose to her cheeks, silently she cursed herself. Surely, she should have known better than to provoke this confrontation with him. The confines of the car had become claustrophobic; his closeness all but overpowered her. But she forced herself to meet his hard, cold gaze. 'You enjoy the sense of power all the same.'

'What power?' The blue eyes narrowed curiously.

'The power to control, to take over people's lives.'

'And whose life have I taken over, would you say?'

She could easily have answered, 'Mine', but with great care she refrained. He was so close she could feel the warmth of him, sense the raw vitality in his taut, hard frame. Involuntarily, she inched her knee away from the long, muscular thigh that threatened to brush against her own. It would be unwise, she sensed instinctively, to draw the exchange on to a more personal plain. 'The lives of the people in Strathbiggin,' she answered levelly.

'To their advantage, I would say.'

'Of course you would. Your type always do.'

A flicker of something crossed his eyes. 'By "my type", you're referring to the Baxters, I presume?'

So he was learning. She smiled without humour. 'Precisely,' she replied.

Inexplicably, the anger left his face. His expression was thoughtful now. He sat back in his seat and regarded her with sudden curiosity. 'They must have done something very terrible to you to make you hate them so much,' he said.

Taken by surprise, Sarah stared down at her hands. 'You're wrong, they've done nothing to me. I hate them for what they are and for what they've done to this community. But, if you must know——' she took a deep breath '—they once did something pretty terrible to someone who's very dear to me.'

He was watching her closely, one arm resting lightly against the steering wheel. 'Carry on,' he encouraged in a quiet voice.

'My Uncle Dougal,' she confided. Then, mildly surprised at herself for opening up to him, she concluded, 'He worked for them as a shepherd for more than fifty years, since he was a boy of thirteen. And at the end of it, when he finally retired, what did he have to show for it?' In a wordless, but utterly explicit gesture, she unclenched her empty hands. 'Nothing, that's what he had. A pension that would scarcely keep a dog, and not even a home to call his own.'

'I don't understand.'

'Then I'll explain. My uncle lived all his life in what's called a tied house in these parts—one, that is, that goes with the job. And, in spite of Baxter's promises that he'd be allowed to go on living in it after he retired, it didn't quite work out like that.' She swallowed, remembering that unhappy time. 'Instead, they simply evicted him. If Dougal's sister hadn't died and left him her cottage and a bit of cash, he would have ended out in the street, for all any of the Baxters cared.'

The blue eyes narrowed, but he didn't speak. Sarah straightened and pushed back her hair. 'And I'm far from being the only one with a tale like that to tell.' She sat back in her seat and glanced at him defensively, remembering how he had so recently been the Baxters' guest. 'However, I've no doubt such disagreeable topics weren't raised over the smoked salmon and fillet steaks the other night.'

Amusement flickered in his eyes. 'I don't recall what we had to eat.'

'Of course. In such captivating company one tends not to notice what's on one's plate.'

A faint smile lingered around his lips. 'The meal was pleasant, as I recall.'

'I'm sure it was.' She smiled sarcastically. 'When it comes to the art of gracious living, there are few who can teach the Baxters anything. For someone as important as yourself, I'm sure they put on quite a show.'

He smiled. 'It was my first taste of Highland hospitality. I was quite impressed.'

It was only then that she remembered Dougal's request—that she invite McCabe round for dinner some night. Feeling suddenly threatened by him, she folded her arms across her chest and deliberately turned away. Highland courtesy or no, it was more than she could bring herself to do.

Hurriedly, she changed the subject. 'Unless there's something else I should see, perhaps we could be getting back. I've a pretty full schedule this afternoon, and I'm already behind as it is.'

He glanced at his watch. 'And I have an appointment at one.' He pushed the car back into gear. 'If it's all right with you, I'll drop you off at the castle gates.'

They drove back the way they had come in silence, each occupied with his own thoughts. As Sarah gazed out at the silent, snow-clad countryside, her feelings were oddly mixed. In a way, she felt reassured. This scheme of his would not, after all, be the vile abomination she had feared. But that very fact disorientated her, for it weakened her ammunition in her fight—and, in spite of what she had learned today, she had no intention of calling a truce.

She glanced with suspicion at the pensive, dark profile at her side. She was still a long way from trusting this man. So she would simply have to use as best she could whatever weapons she had left.

As they drew up outside the castle gates, he slid a large buff envelope from under his seat. 'These are the photographs,' he told her. 'Make sure your editor uses them.'

Damned martinet! She snatched the envelope from his hand and started to open up the door. 'Will there be anything else?' she demanded in a sarcastic tone.

'Not for now. I'll let you know. Until the weather clears, we can't get started, I'm afraid.' He frowned and glanced up at the sky. 'And it looks like more snow to me.'

It looked like more snow to Sarah as well. As she climbed down from the car, she intentionally caught his eye. 'That's too bad,' she remarked. And smiled, pleased.

He held her gaze. 'Don't count your chickens,' he advised. 'I'm sure I'll find something for you to do.' Then leaned across quickly and added with a warning smile as he started to pull the car door shut, 'In the meantime, just you make sure you do as good a job on this report as you did on the last. I'll be keeping an eye on you.' And all Sarah could do was curse him under her breath as the car door slammed and he accelerated off.

She was still cursing when she got back to the office for a quick lunch of coffee and sandwiches at her desk. Keeping an eye on her, indeed! He virtually had her on a leash!

'There's a call for you, Sarah! I'm putting it through!'

She had scarcely finished eating when Tom called across, and she snatched her extension to her ear. '*Strathbiggin Gazette* reporters. Sarah Drummond here.'

'Miss Drummond, I'm afraid it's me again.' At the sound of Brett McCabe's voice, she felt her heart sink, and it sank even farther as he went on, 'I'm sorry to bother you, but there's been an unexpected turn of events.'

Whatever it was, it could only be bad. She took a deep breath. 'Oh, yes?' she said.

To add insult to injury, she detected a note of wry amusement in his voice as he went on, 'Just after I left you, I took a wrong turning and lost my way——'

That was the good news, apparently, but the bad news was still to come.

'—I had to stop and ask directions from an old man out walking his dog——'

Her heart turned over wretchedly, anticipating what was coming next.

'What a coincidence——' He paused, milking the moment. 'Guess who it turned out to be?'

'I couldn't,' she lied.

'It was your Uncle Dougal, no less. Wasn't that a lucky chance?'

Sarah's grip tightened around the phone. It wasn't so much a lucky chance, she feared, as an outright calamity.

'Well, we got talking, and very interesting it was, too.' Again the note of wry amusement as, with evident relish, he came to the point. 'As a matter of fact, he kindly suggested that we continue our conversation over dinner some night. Tomorrow night, to be precise. If that's all right with you?'

What could she say? Without even bothering to try, it seemed, he'd outsmarted her again.

With a superhuman effort, she bit back her rage and counted, very slowly, up to ten. Then she took a deep breath and lied through her teeth. 'Tomorrow would be perfect,' she said.

CHAPTER FOUR

THE whole house was filled with delicious smells.

From the kitchen, the aroma of roast venison mingled with the subtle tangs of bramble sauce and home-made cock-a-leekie soup, while a bowl of fragrant vanilla cream stood ready for the pear compôte. Through in the dining-room, a couple of bottles of red French wine, already decorked, sat waiting on the oak sideboard, while, from the ready-laid table with its embroidered linen cloth, a centrepiece of golden crysanthemums breathed its delicate perfume into the air.

Sarah had really gone to town. She'd started the preparations last night after work and had only just finished an hour ago. Now, fresh from a long, luxurious bath, she slipped off the bright pink towelling robe and draped it across the bed, padded across the carpet to her dressing-table on bare feet and, in a rare gesture of sheer extravagance, sprayed herself from head to toe with Coco, her favourite scent.

As she reached into her underwear drawer for her prettiest lace bra and pants, she glanced at her reflection in the mirror and wryly shook her head. The power of positive thinking, she smiled to herself. Apparently, there were no limits to the wonders it could achieve.

Her initial reaction to Dougal's invitation to

McCabe had been far from positive.

'How could you?' she'd accused her uncle. 'Behind my back!'

Though that had hardly been fair, as he'd reminded her. 'I told you I wanted to invite him here—and I asked you to do it for me. Unfortunately, you forgot.' He smiled a knowing smile at her, believing no such thing. 'But don't worry, lass,' he'd soothed, 'the evening will be no burden to you. Mrs Campbell will do the cooking. She's already said she would.'

But Sarah wasn't having that. 'Oh, no,' she'd protested firmly. 'That's my job!' Any guest at the cottage, however unwelcome, was her responsibility.

And the truth was, once she'd got herself in the mood, she'd actually quite enjoyed all the preparations. She and Dougal had few occasions to entertain, and she rather welcomed the opportunity to show off her prowess as a cook. So, tonight, she had decided, would be a feast. A dinner to remember for all concerned. Tonight, the detested Brett McCabe would find out what *true* Highland hospitality really was.

The evening was also a rare opportunity for Sarah to dress up. Not out of any desire to impress McCabe, but for the simple, feminine pleasure of looking good. As she lifted down the slinky, jewel-blue dress with its wide scoop neck and figure-skimming lines, she felt a lift of pleasure at the prospect of wearing it. She'd bought it last year—in another extravagant moment, on a shopping trip to Edinburgh—and, apart from an airing on Dougal's birthday, it had hung in her wardrobe ever since. Tonight would see its baptism by fire!

She glanced at her watch as she sat down at the dressing-table and opened up her make-up box. It was a quarter to eight. Another fifteen minutes, and he was due to arrive. Quickly, she smoothed some eyeshadow in a soft shade of grey over her lids, and opened her wide hazel eyes even wider with a couple of strokes of the mascara wand. A subtle sweep of blusher—not too much—followed by a light application of transparent coral lipgloss and she was done. Her short, bouncy auburn hair brushed easily into place and, with a smile, she got to her feet.

The dress felt gorgeous as she slipped it on, and one glance in the mirror confirmed how outrageously good it looked. The colour was perfect and the simple, classic lines wickedly flattered her slender figure. She slid her feet into high-heeled black suede courts with neat bows at the front, crossed to the dressing table once more and opened up her jewel-box. Then, with a twist of emotion, she lifted out the pretty lapis lazuli ear-rings that had belonged to her mother—and to her grandmother before that—and proudly slid them into place. A final halo of Coco and she was ready for anything.

Dougal was waiting by the drawing-room fire, looking like a country gent in his best tweed suit, and his face lit up with pride as he caught sight of her. 'You're a stunner, lass,' he smiled, and squeezed her hand affectionately as she bent to kiss him on the cheek. 'I'm fair proud of you.'

She was in the kitchen, warming the soup and putting the finishing touches to the roast, when she heard the Range Rover arrive outside. It was two minutes past eight precisely, according to the kitchen clock. He might be a boor in other respects, but Brett McCabe was a well-mannered guest.

She whipped off her apron, ran her fingers through her hair and waited for the bell to ring. 'I'll get it!' she called through to Dougal as she hurried out into the hall. Then she straightened her shoulders and reminded herself firmly of the resolution she'd made. At all costs, she would be polite to him. If it killed her. For Dougal's sake.

Pinning a false smile to her face, she opened the door.'Good evening, Mr McCabe!'

But the smile died instantly on her lips and something very peculiar happened to her insides as she found herself staring into his face. Never in her life before had she seen a man look quite this good.

He was wearing a dark navy cashmere overcoat, loosely open to reveal a matching navy suit and crisp white shirt beneath. And the bright silk tie at his neck was the exact same colour as his eyes. In the light from the hallway, the lines of his face were strong and dark, oddly compelling somehow. And there was something faintly disarming about the freshly fallen snowflakes that glistened in the jet-black hair.

'Good evening, Miss Drummond,' he replied.

In sudden, mild confusion, Sarah dropped her eyes. 'Come in,' she invited, stepping aside. And closed the door quickly as he came inside.

He slipped off his coat and glanced round for somewhere to deposit it.

'Thank you. I'll take that.' As she reached out to take it from him, feeling the warm, soft weight of it in her arms, she was aware of the clean, cool masculine scent that rose to her nostrils from the expensive cloth.

The suit he wore was evidently expensive, too, the sharp broad-shouldered lines lending an air of easy, sophisticated elegance to the lean, hard, muscular physique beneath. Yet he wore it as casually and as naturally as his more customary leather jerkin and jeans. Somehow, she sensed, he was a man who would automatically command the tone of whatever social situation he was in.

'Welcome!' Dougal had appeared in the drawing-room doorway, a broad smile of welcome on his face.

McCabe stepped forward to shake the old man's outstretched hand. 'Good to see you again.'

And Sarah took her opportunity to withdraw. 'I've a couple of things to see to in the kitchen,' she demurred, glad of the excuse to make herself scarce.

'You go ahead, lass.' Dougal ushered his guest into the drawing-room. 'While we're waiting for you, Mr McCabe and I will warm ourselves up with a pre-prandial dram.'

She deposited the coat on the bed in her room and hurried back to the cock-a-leekie soup. Back there, just for a moment, her composure had slipped a bit, and she could sense a sudden tension crackling in the air. It was always the same when McCabe was around. His presence knocked her out of sync.

With a flash of irritation, she shoved the soup-plates under the grill and resolved to leave McCabe in Dougal's hands tonight. The less she had to do with him, the better it would be all round. And anyway, she rationalised, he was really Dougal's guest.

Her uncle seemed happy to oblige. A reserved man

by nature, tonight he appeared to be in his element, chatting away, relaxed and easy, as the three of them gathered round the table in the tiny cottage dining-room.

'We're rather tucked away here in the wilds,' he observed as he broke a piece of crusty bread and drank a mouthful of the delicious soup. 'I hope you didn't have any trouble finding us?'

'None at all.' The blue eyes glanced across at Sarah. 'The directions your niece gave me were very clear.'

A pat on the head from McCabe was something she didn't need. She met his gaze with a cool, blank look. 'I'm surprised you needed directions at all,' she informed him censoriously. 'We're on the same road as the Baxters after all—and by now you must know your way there almost like the back of your hand.'

One eyebrow lifted in amusement at her. 'Don't worry, I'm learning,' he said. And held her eyes for a moment more as Dougal hurried to intervene.

'You must find it all a bit strange over here,' he offered on a more neutral note. 'I expect they do things differently, on a grander scale, where you come from?'

McCabe nodded and laid down his spoon. 'In a lot of ways, you're right. The pace is a great deal slower here. There isn't the same sense of urgency you would tend to find back home.'

Dougal nodded agreeably. 'This is an older country,' he observed. 'Perhaps we've grown a little tired.'

'Maybe.' The younger man threw him a sympathetic smile. 'But there's a lot to be said for the old ways, I find. It makes a very pleasant change.'

'You find us quaint, Mr McCabe?' Sarah couldn't resist it. His attitude was patronising in the extreme. She ignored the look of displeasure on Dougal's face as she went on, 'No doubt you'll have lots of amusing tales to entertain the folks back home?'

He sat back and regarded her with a superior smile. 'A few,' he answered, unperturbed. 'Not to mention one or two rather amusing clips of film!'

Touché. She pursed her lips and said no more. This could prove to be dangerous ground.

He paused to savour her unease before leaning forward again and resting his arms on the table edge. The heavy, pale gold cuff-links glistened in the candlelight. 'But, to answer your question—no, I don't find you quaint. My interest in your country goes a great deal deeper than that.' His eyes swivelled round to include Dougal now as he went on, 'It so happens that my forefathers were Highland folk. From Fort William, to be exact. We may have been born on the opposite sides of the ocean, but our roots are still the same.'

It was not a notion Sarah cared for in the least. McCabe was an interloper and an alien, as different from herself as chalk from cheese. She shot him a disapproving look. 'People grow away from their roots,' she pointed out.

'That's why I wanted to come back. To re-establish contact, if you like.' His eyes locked with hers, deep and unexpectedly intense. 'Building the centre is my way of doing that.'

She smiled a disbelieving smile. 'So you're a sentimentalist at heart?' Anyone who believed that was capable of believing anything?

'Now there's something I want to talk to you about.' Diplomatically, Dougal cut in. 'The centre.' His eyes were fastened on McCabe. 'There are a couple of little questions I'd like you to clear up for me.'

Sarah took that as her cue to go through to the kitchen and see to the roast. She had no desire to stick around and listen to McCabe extolling the virtues of his wretched scheme. He would never convince her it was for the good of Strathbiggin, not if he tried for a thousand years.

But he seemed to be doing a pretty good job of talking Dougal round. By the time she returned with the second course, the old man was nodding thoughtfully as McCabe explained, '. . . What you say about the building jobs being short-term is true, of course. But consider the crews of maintenance workers we'll have to employ long-term. And all the sports instructors and admin staff. These jobs will be increasing in number all the time as the centre expands.'

As one of her favourite arguments was shot down in flames, Sarah laid the roast down on the table with a thud. 'Perhaps you'd do the honours, Mr McCabe?' she invited caustically. And, with lethal politeness, extended the carving implements to him, only just managing to bite back, 'You're such an expert at carving things up!'

'My pleasure.' Watching her closely, he rose to his feet and his fingers grazed hers momentarily as he took the bone handles in his hand. As something in her seem to freeze, the blue eyes locked with hers. 'I think it's time we dropped the formalities, don't you? I'd really feel much happier if you'd both call me Brett.'

'As you prefer.' She sat down woodenly and lowered her gaze, confused and embarrassed by the sudden, acute discomfort she felt. She watched the dark profile resentfully from the corner of her eye as her uncle responded with a genial smile, 'I'm Dougal to my friends.'

Brett McCabe would never be a friend of hers, whatever name she called him by.

Nevertheless, the evening was a fair success. Sarah's efforts in the kitchen were roundly praised—and, more to the point, consumed with gusto by both men. As the wine flowed, the conversation moved along with ease. And one thing was established beyond any doubt. Dougal Drummond and Brett McCabe got on like a house on fire. As, over the pear compôte and vanilla cream, they launched into a lively discussion on the intricacies of catching trout, Sarah watched the old man's animated face with mingled pleasure and regret. It was almost as though he'd found the son he'd always longed for but never had. What a pity he couldn't have found a slightly more worthy substitute.

All the unaccustomed excitement soon began to tell on the old man. As Sarah cleared away the coffee things, she could see that he looked tired. He sighed and stretched and shook his head at Brett. 'If you'll excuse me, I think I'd better turn in now. It's long past my bedtime,' he smiled. Creakily, he got to his feet and held out one weatherbeaten hand. 'It's been a pleasure,' he said. 'I hope you'll come again.'

'The pleasure's mine.' Respectfully, McCabe stood up too, and, warmly, the two men shook hands.

'Sarah will look after you now. Go through to the fire and have another glass of Glenmorangie.'

Studiously, Sarah avoided McCabe's eyes and prayed that he'd turn the offer down. With Dougal around, his company had been just about bearable. At least the old man's presence had kept them from each other's throats. But, now that they were to be left alone, it was really better that he go—as surely he was capable of seeing for himself.

Not so. Insensitive to the bitter end, he turned to Sarah with a smile. 'I can think of nothing nicer,' he said.

They went through to the drawing-room as Dougal padded off to bed, Sarah reflecting with annoyance that she didn't even have the washing up to use as an excuse to absent herself. Tomorrow was one of Mrs Campbell's days, and the good woman had insisted that they leave all the clearing up to her. She poured a moderate measure of the old malt whisky into a glass and handed it to Brett.

'Won't you join me?' The blue eyes were on her face as she made no move to pour one for herself. 'Surely you don't expect me to drink alone?'

She was standing stiffly in front of the fire, loath to humour him in any way. 'I'm afraid I don't like whisky,' she replied contrarily.

'Have something else.' He smiled reasonably at her and gestured to the armchair next to his. 'Then come and sit down here and talk to me—unless you'd rather go to bed.'

She shrugged. 'I'm not particularly tired.' And

it was true, oddly enough. In spite of the long, busy day she'd had, she felt quite startlingly fresh and alert. A little *too* alert, perhaps, she couldn't help thinking to herself. As though all her physical and mental faculties were suddenly on guard. She could feel the tension that had assailed her earlier creeping over her again. With a gesture, she crossed back to the drinks cabinet and took out a bottle of Drambuie. Perhaps a thimbleful of liqueur would help her to relax a bit.

She crossed to the sofa opposite him, declining the armchair at his side, and, arranging her slim legs demurely, sat down without a word. If he wanted to be sociable, let him do the work!

He continued to watch her calmly as she sipped a mouthful from her glass. 'I don't think I mentioned it,' he said at last, 'but you're looking extraordinarily lovely tonight.'

It was as though he'd pulled the rug from under her feet. She gulped and shot back gauchely, 'I bet you say that to all your hostesses!' And felt instantly annoyed at herself.

'No, not all.' Then he went on to unsettle her even more as he added with a smile, 'You're also, if I may say so, an excellent cook. That was the best meal I've tasted in years.'

Sarah threw him a damning look. 'You're wasting your time, you know. All this New-World charm may impress some of your more gullible acquaintances, but I'm afraid you don't fool me.'

As he sat back in his chair and took a long, slow mouthful of his drink, he looked at once utterly composed, yet totally relaxed. The unbuttoned front of his navy jacket had slipped back to reveal the crisp white shirt, and the long, athletic legs were stretched out casually in front of him. He regarded her over the top of his glass with mild amusement in his eyes. 'You should learn to accept compliments more gracefully, Sarah. Don't be so defensive all the time.'

So, he was trying to patronise her again! She flashed him an angry look. 'I don't need lessons in etiquette from you, thank you all the same!'

He smiled a faintly mocking smile. 'I'm not suggesting that you do.' He cradled the whisky glass in his hand. 'But why don't you try and relax for a change?'

Because she couldn't. It was as simple as that. His presence threw her into a state of unease and she seemed to have no control over it. As the long, brown fingers tightened around the glass and slowly raised it to his lips, she was aware of the blue eyes watching her; taking in at one leisurely glance the smooth, creamy skin of her neck and throat, then dropping to graze her slim, poised legs.

'At the risk of rubbing you up the wrong way again, I have another piece of praise.'

'Oh?' Illogically, her stomach tensed, fearing some unwanted intimacy.

He paused and rolled the amber liquid round in his glass as his eyes lifted once more to her face. 'And, believe me, this is praise indeed, coming from the likes of me.' He smiled as a faint trace of self-mockery crept into his voice. 'I don't know if you're aware of it, but you really are a damned good journalist.'

So, it was only that. She felt relieved, though her tone was wary as she replied, 'Please don't judge me on that rubbish I've been writing for you. That's PR stuff, not journalism.'

He shook his head. 'I wasn't judging you on that. I've been looking through some back copies of the *Gazette*, and I'm really quite impressed by some of the work you've done.'

Sarah fingered her half-empty glass and raised it self-consciously to her lips. 'Just routine,' she assured him hurriedly, suddenly feeling both flattered and irked. 'Nothing very world-shattering ever happens around here, as you've probably gathered by now.'

'That's not the point. What you do, you do well.' He raised an interested eyebrow at her. 'Have you ever thought of moving—to a bigger paper in a bigger town?'

'Not really. I like it here.' And she did—though secretly she'd often dreamed of spreading her wings elsewhere. But it was hard somehow to make the break, especially since Dougal needed her. Defiantly, she met Brett's eyes, resenting him prodding so close to her dreams. 'I'm just a small-town girl,' she acidly reminded him. 'Not a big-city slicker like you.'

He laughed at that and leaned back against the antimacassar at his head, his dark hair contrasting sharply with the pale linen of the cloth. 'Nothing could be further from the truth, I'm afraid. 'I'm no big-city slicker, just a country boy at heart.'

He'd dropped similar hints over dinner when he'd talked about the ranch he owned, but Sarah had been faintly sceptical, as she still was now, as he went on, 'The little town in western Ontario, where I grew up, was less than a quarter of the size of Strathbiggin.

Right up in the mountains. A real hick place. I didn't even set foot in Toronto till I was seventeen.'

She regarded him with curiosity. 'But you've left all that behind you now?'

'Not really. I still hanker after the wide open spaces. That's why I like to get away to the Lakes and spend some time on the ranch whenever I can. To relax, to escape from the hubbub of the city, to smell a bit of fresh country air. That's also why it suits me so well here.' He eyed her. 'I can understand your reluctance to leave.'

Perhaps he could. 'It's home,' she said.

'Wherever you go, it will always be home—just like that little place where I was born will always be home to me.'

Her eyes scanned his face. 'Do you ever go back?' she asked.

'Frequently. My parents are still living there.'

Parents? She blinked at him. It was odd to imagine him possessing anything quite so mundane.

'My father's the local schoolmaster,' he volunteered before she could ask.

Curiouser and curiouser. Such modest roots. Surely, if Brett McCabe had to have a father at all, he'd have one who was president of the Bank of Canada—at the very least! 'That's funny,' she observed, suddenly thrown for something to say. 'My aunt, whose cottage this used to be, was a schoolteacher, too.' She smiled, remembering. 'I think Uncle Dougal had hopes at first that I might follow in her footsteps one day. And I thought about it,' she confessed. Then couldn't resist adding, tongue in cheek, 'But I'm afraid that prying nature of mine finally got the better of me.'

'Perhaps we should both be glad of it.' He smiled at her ambiguously. 'We would never have struck up this pleasant little partnership of ours if you'd become a schoolteacher.'

For a moment their eyes locked, and it was almost like a physical clash. Feeling her stomach suddenly clench, Sarah tore her gaze away. 'What about you?' she wanted to know, abruptly turning the subject round. 'How did you get into your line of business?'

'Entirely by accident—the way all the best things in life seem to happen.' He smiled and ran a hand over his thick, dark hair. 'My parents were all for me becoming an engineer, but I'm afraid I got side-tracked in my final year.' He smiled again. 'They weren't too pleased at first, but they've come round to the idea now.'

Sarah burst out laughing, catching the twinkle in his eye. 'I should think they would!' From schoolmaster to multi-millionaire landowner in one generation was no mean feat! She threw him a teasing glance. 'And were you the only one in the family to make good?' she asked.

'It depends what you mean by making good. My two older sisters are happily married, one to a dentist and the other to a traffic cop. I'm an uncle five times over.' He grinned, apparently proud of the fact. 'How about you? Are you an aunt?'

She shook her head. 'I'm an only child, I'm afraid. The only real family I have is Dougal.'

'What about all those people over there?' He leaned forward a little in his seat and nodded at the group of family photographs that were arranged on the bookcase behind her head. 'Are any of these your relatives?'

Sarah swivelled round and shrugged. 'A few,' she answered evasively, reluctant to encourage him.

'May I see?'

'I don't think——'

'I'd like to. Really. I'm interested.'

There was no polite way to say no, and no good reason for doing so. With a sigh, she got to her feet and unwillingly lifted a few of them down. There were so many precious memories locked within those frames. A lifetime of love and laughter and loss. Not to be shared with just anyone.

She passed the first one to him: a tall, upright man in a kilt, with a dainty, smiling woman at his side. 'This is Uncle Dougal, and Aunt Minnie, his wife. It was taken on holiday on the Isle of Skye.'

Brett took it. 'He was a good-looking man,' he observed. And Sarah watched him from the corner of her eye as he bent with interest to study it. In the soft glow of the fire the dark brow was smooth, the mouth full and strong, and she found herself noticing for the very first time the slight indentation in his chin. He turned round to look at her suddenly. 'I'm told it's a very romantic place, Skye. One day, I'd like to visit it.'

Bonnie Prince Charlie and all that. 'Then you should,' she told him. And added, half disbelieving, half sincere, 'If you're really serious about unearthing those roots of yours, it's one place you definitely ought to see.' Then, quickly, she handed over the next photograph to him. 'This was my mother when she was young.'

An extremely beautiful young girl with a head of wild, bright auburn hair was smiling up at him. 'She's lovely. She looks just like you.'

'So they say.'

'And she's wearing your ear-rings.'

'Is she?' Sarah leaned closer to check, mildly surprised at his sharp eye. 'I'd forgotten that.' And she raised a hand self-consciously to touch the lapis studs in her ears.

'They're very unusual. I've been admiring them all night.'

She was standing far too close to him. She could almost feel his warmth, the strong male pulse in him. And the blue of his eyes was startling against the thick black lashes and the tan of his skin. Almost clumsily, she stepped away, lengthening the space that separated them. 'And these are my parents,' she said, almost thrusting the final photograph at him. 'It was taken on their wedding day.'

He sat back in his seat and glanced up at her with a curious smile. 'This will be you soon, I suppose?'

'Then you suppose wrong.' She regarded him levelly, sensing an edge of chauvinism in his remark. 'I'm more interested in pursuing my career.'

He smiled, amused. 'Why not have both? That's what I intend to do.'

So, he was in the market for a wife. She crossed to the sofa, but didn't sit down. 'Who's the lucky lady, then?' she enquired in a sarcastic voice.

He looked straight back at her and laid the pile of photos down. 'I'm afraid I haven't found her yet. As a matter of fact, I thought I might find her here.'

For some odd, inexplicable reason, an image of

Amanda Baxter flashed instantly to Sarah's mind. Tall and blonde and haughty, with that familiar sneer in her eye. Unable to resist, she flashed the challenge at him. 'What about your charming hostess of the other night?' she asked. 'I'm sure she's in the market, too.'

'Amanda?' He looked at her in slight surprise and smiled an enigmatic smile. 'She's certainly a good-looking girl.'

'And comes from a good family, too.' But then, so did Lucretia Borgia—though she bit that observation back.

'You'd recommend her, would you?'

'Ideal. She'd come with a handsome dowry, no doubt, and all the right connections, too.' She was being bitchy, for no reason at all, but somehow she couldn't stop herself. 'You really ought to consider her. You two would make an ideal pair.'

His eyes swept briefly over her face, their expression unreadable. 'It's getting late,' he said suddenly, and started to stand up. 'I think it's time I called it a day.'

She felt suddenly as jumpy as a flea. A pulse in her temple had started to throb and her throat felt parched and dry. She moved abruptly towards the door. 'I'll get your coat,' she said.

She almost ran the short distance to her room, then paused for a moment to catch her breath and try to still the sudden frantic beating of her anxious heart. What on earth had come over her? She didn't normally behave like this. She snatched up the cashmere coat. She was tired, that was all it was. Once he was gone and she was safely tucked up in bed, she'd start to feel sane again.

He was standing in the doorway as she turned round, quite still and silently watching her. And her heart leapt to her throat as an unknown fear assaulted her. Numbly, clutching the warm coat to her chest, she stepped forward hesitantly. Then came to a stop an arm's length away and held it out to him. 'Here,' was all she managed to say. She was suddenly trembling from head to toe.

As the coat slipped from her nerveless fingers and fell with a soft swish to the floor, he made no move to pick it up. Instead, without a word, he stepped forward and took her hand and drew her gently into his arms.

It felt like falling into a dream. As her eyes focused foolishly on the blue silk tie, she was half convinced at the back of her mind that, if she could just find the will to blink, like some apparition, he would disappear. But she couldn't blink. She couldn't move. As his fingers softly tilted her chin, she tried to swallow, but could not. Then it all seemed to happen like a slow-motion film unfolding before her eyes as the apparition, warm and real, inexorably closed in on her and she felt his mouth come down on hers.

His kiss was as soft as a butterfly's wing, his lips like gossamer against hers. And she seemed to be floating in his arms. Out of her body. Out on a cloud. As his hand pressed against the small of her back, moulding her to him, she felt a shaft of raw excitement flare deep in her loins. And the breath seemed to leave her body in a shuddering, helpless sigh as his fingers softly laced her hair to caress the sensitive nape of her neck.

It was a wild, mad, crazy moment, sweeping all logic and reason aside. As the pressure of his lips increased, devouring and fiercely sensual, Sarah's paper-thin resistance was on the verge of caving in. There was a fire in his kiss that awakened some deep urge in her. It tore at her senses and laid bare her soul.

Gently then, he started to prise her lips apart and she felt the heat of his tongue on her teeth. And a violent longing ripped through her, the like of which she had never experienced before. Every naked nerve-end in her body was crying out for him, every instinct in her clamouring to respond.

But it was wrong. In a panic of desperation, she pulled herself free. 'No!' Her hand flew to her throbbing mouth as she stumbled awkwardly away. And a blistering, outraged fury raged at him from her eyes as she hissed out in a warning voice, 'Don't ever dare do that again!'

For a long, electric moment, he didn't move. Just stood there in the doorway, eyes narrowed, watching her. Then, abruptly, he shrugged and bent to retrieve the fallen coat. 'As you wish,' he answered quietly. Then he swung the coat lightly over his shoulders and turned sharply away.

In a tumult of confused emotion, Sarah watched him cross the hall. She was trembling so hard, she could barely stand. She had to lean for support on the wall.

He pulled the front door open and paused to look round at her. A dark and dangerous figure silhouetted against the wintry sky. And his tone was chilling as he bade her, 'Goodnight. And thank you for your hospitality.'

She didn't move a muscle until the door had closed and she heard the Range Rover's engine rev, then drive away across the snow. Then, with a helpless, violent sob that spoke of all the anguish in her soul, she turned and laid her face against the wall and dissolved into a bitter flood of tears.

CHAPTER FIVE

THE SNOW showed no sign of clearing yet. It lay like a fine white mantle across the land, keeping the farmers from their ploughs and the cows locked in the barns. And, most importantly of all, as far as Sarah was concerned, grounding the excavators and cranes that were poised to start moving in on Brett McCabe's estate.

Four days had passed since that evening which had ended so disastrously, and she hadn't set eyes on him again since. He had sent round a note of thanks for the dinner the following morning, along with a bottle of Dougal's favourite Glenmorangie, and had rung the cottage once when Sarah was out. Whether he was deliberately avoiding her or not, she couldn't guess—though she rated the likelihood quite high. No doubt, he regretted that momentary lapse and was allowing the dust time to settle again.

In the meantime, so she had heard, he'd been establishing more likely links. A couple of evenings ago, he'd been seen at the Neuk Inn, the area's fashionable eating place, sharing a candlelit corner table with none other than Amanda Baxter, the laird's daughter herself. So, after all, he had taken her advice, Sarah decided with relief.

That suited her just perfectly—as well as going to prove her point. He was definitely of their ilk, and birds of a feather flock together. Not, alas, that that meant she had finally seen the back of him. It was just a matter of time, she knew, till he descended on her once more.

'Sarah! I've been looking all over for you!'

It was half-past six on a Monday evening and Sarah was parking her car in the *Gazette* car park when a familiar voice called out. She climbed out with a smile as sports editor Tom came hurrying across the tarmac to her. 'What's up?' she wanted to know, praying that it wasn't some after-hours job. She'd been out on assignments for most of the day and was looking forward to an evening in front of the fire.

Tom shook his grey head and smiled at her. 'Don't worry. Just an invitation to Susie's third birthday party on Saturday afternoon. Morag said I was to give you plenty of warning, before you fixed up something else.'

Fat chance of that! Sarah's Saturday afternoons were generally spent shopping or walking the dog. 'I'd love to come,' she assured Tom warmly. He and his wife had come to parenthood a little late in life, and their bright little daughter was the apple of their eye. Sarah was flattered to share with them the pleasures of family life. 'You can tell Morag I'll definitely be there. I'll even come round early and give her a hand.'

'Good girl.' He glanced at his watch. 'I'm off to cover the snooker final. I'd better get there before it starts.'

Sarah couldn't resist pulling his leg. 'You wouldn't want to miss the first round of refreshments, would you?' she laughed.

'Definitely not,' he smiled back at her. Then added

as he started to move away, 'Drop round for an hour if you've nothing better to do. It promises to be a good match.'

'I might. I'm just nipping up to the office to make a couple of quick calls and see if there are any messages for me.' She turned up the collar of her coat. 'Anyway, enjoy yourself. And I'll see you tomorrow if I don't see you tonight.'

A hum of busy concentration filled the office as she walked in. And, as always, it struck Sarah that, in the life of a daily newspaper, this was the most exciting time of the day—when the sum of all the day's activities was drawn together to make the whole. She exchanged a smile with a couple of reporters who sat battering out last-minute stories at their desks, while a row of furiously efficient subs wrestled with ever-growing piles of printout from the agency machines.

There were no urgent messages waiting for her, Sarah was greatly relieved to see, and it took her less than fifteen minutes to make the calls she had to make. With a sigh of relief, she locked her desk and packed her bag, ready to go. Maybe she would join Tom for an hour.

It was precisely at that moment that the phone on her desk began to ring. And somehow she knew before she even picked it up that her plans were about to be knocked on the head.

'Good evening,' he purred. 'You're just the girl I'm looking for.'

At the sound of Brett McCabe's voice, an unexpected jolt tore through her, catching her totally unawares. For one sharp, uncomfortable moment, she was back in the bedroom with him, trapped like

a prisoner in his arms. She swallowed and managed
to inform him in a cool, tight voice, 'I was just
leaving, as a matter of fact.'

'Then I'm glad I caught you.' He paused. 'I have a
proposition to make.'

Sarah sighed and sank down despondently in her
chair. The reprieve she'd been enjoying had come to
an end. It looked as if Brett McCabe was about to start
breathing down her neck again.

She listened in silence for the next few minutes
while he explained what he had in mind. Then she
informed him, when he'd finished, 'I'm afraid I can't
agree to that without having a word with McAndrew
first.'

'Is he there?'

'I think so.'

'Then speak to him now. And phone me back
immediately. I'll be waiting for your call.'

As the phone went dead, Sarah cursed him under
her breath. Why did he have to come along and spoil
a perfectly pleasant evening? Then, resignedly, she
got to her feet and trudged across the reporters' room
to the editor's office at the other end. There was no
point in trying to resist. She was the one who'd made
her bed, and now he was making her lie on it.

As she stuck her head around his door, McAndrew
glanced up at her over the top of his steel-rimmed
spectacles. 'Come in, Sarah. Sit down. What can I do
for you?'

Say no to the request I'm about to make, she
thought to herself with irony. Though somehow she
doubted that he would. She smiled stiffly and sat
down, crossing her long, slim legs. 'It's McCabe,'

she started to explain. 'He's just been on the phone. He wants me to do a story about this bothy up at Cairn Ban that he's had converted into an overnight shelter for mountaineers. He suggested I meet the couple who're going to run it and do an interview with them.'

McAndrew nodded approvingly, just as she'd feared. 'Sounds like a good idea. And when would he like you to set it up?'

'He's already set it up. For tomorrow.' She made a face. 'The trouble is, I've a couple of other jobs on tomorrow as it is. It would mean I'd have to cancel them.'

'How important are they?'

'One's the opening of the new nursery school. Mrs Baxter will be there. And the other's an interview with that French pianist who's visiting. It's the only chance I'll have to talk to him.'

McAndrew scribbled a couple of notes on the notepad in front of him and, ever hopeful, Sarah held her breath. But the next instant, her hopes were dashed as he instructed, 'You stick with the McCabe project, that's the most important thing. I'll get one of the other reporters to cover the other two.' Then a brief frown creased his brow as a sudden thought occurred to him. 'How are you going to get up there with all this snow?'

This was the choicest part, the part that really bothered her. 'McCabe said he'd take me in his car. He's got a four-wheel drive.' She shot a desperate glance at her boss. 'I think I ought to take along a photographer. We're definitely going to need photographs.'

But McAndrew shook his head. 'Can't spare one tomorrow, I'm afraid. You'll have to take along a camera and do the photographs yourself.'

So she was to be stuck alone with Brett McCabe for the entire day. Sarah shuddered inwardly.

'Can you handle that?'

She nodded. 'Sure.' The photographs were no problem at all. After all, she'd done it before. It was the rest of the package that troubled her.

As she made her way back to her desk, suddenly in no mood for snooker, Kevin, the young sub, hurried past. 'Cheer up, Sarah,' he grinned. 'It might never happen, you know!'

She managed a pale smile in return. How little he knew! Then, gritting her teeth, she sat down at her desk, took a deep breath and picked up the phone.

Brett collected her from the office next morning at nine-thirty sharp. It was a good hour's drive up the narrow, twisty road that wound its way half-way up the mountainside to Cairn Ban. An hour, that was, when the weather was good. In the present snowy conditions, it could easily take half as long again. 'And I want to make sure we're back before dark,' he'd advised her over the telephone. At this time of the year the days were short.

Dressed in a heavy blue anorak and red wool sweater over his jeans, he seemed in an almost jaunty mood as she climbed into the Range Rover beside him and they set off. Like her, he'd evidently swept right out of his mind that unfortunate incident of the kiss.

As they made their way speedily through the

outskirts of the town, heading for the mountain road, he flicked a curious glance at her. 'So, Sarah,' he asked, 'what have you been up to since I saw you last?'

'Nothing much.' She avoided looking at his face, her eyes fixed instead on the strong, tanned hands that lightly, but firmly, controlled the steering wheel. And, as she sat back in her seat, she was glad she was wearing what was very probably the least sexy outfit she possessed—a pair of baggy oatmeal cords and a high-necked Aran pullover. For, belatedly, it had crossed her mind that the slinky blue dress she'd worn for dinner that night might have given him the wrong idea. From now on, she'd be making very sure she didn't get her signals crossed.

She detached her eyes abruptly from his hands and stared out of the window, eyes straight ahead. 'I've been extremely busy at work,' she informed him, deliberately distant.

'I'm glad to hear it,' he smiled. 'No time for extra-curricular activities.' Then he added, as irritatedly she bit her lip, 'How's the petition coming along?'

It wasn't—as he probably realised full well. Since her article in the *Gazette*, and the couple of interviews he'd done on local radio, public opinion had swung even more sharply his way. She'd even had a handful of signatories requesting to have their names removed. Though she wasn't about to admit that to him. Even less the fact that her own enthusiasm for the venture had suddenly started to sag a bit.

'I'm still working on it,' she snapped.

He simply smiled, quite unperturbed. 'We've been pretty busy, too, recruiting additional staff. I must have interviewed about fifty people over the past three days.'

'But still found time to acquaint yourself with some of our more exclusive eating places.' The remark had a distinctly cutting edge, and she wished she'd kept it to herself. Where he chose to eat was not of the slightest concern to her. Besides, it sounded rather as though she'd been keeping tabs on him.

Perhaps he thought so, too, for he raised an eyebrow in mild surprise. 'You're referring to my visit to the Neuk Inn, I take it? An excellent establishment.'

'So I'm told.' Personally, she'd never been. 'And no doubt your companion guided you expertly through the menu,' she added scathingly, knowing she shouldn't have said that either, but somehow unable to stop herself. For good measure, she turned and fixed him with a caustic smile. 'I'm so glad you two get along so well.'

'Glad, but surely not surprised.' As he met her gaze, the wide mouth quirked in a superior smile. 'After all, you were the one who pointed out that she was my kind of girl.'

A few miles out of town the road conditions grew markedly worse. Solid drifts, in some places more than six feet high, lined either side of the road in an impenetrable, glistening wall. It was like driving through a bobsleigh run! And it would be much worse farther up the glen, where the snowfalls were always heavier.

Yet, though with any other driver Sarah might have felt nervous, with Brett she felt totally unperturbed. It was clear from the way he handled the car that he was accustomed to such driving conditions—and probably a great deal worse—back home in his native Canada.

As they came up round the back of the loch and started their slow and winding ascent, he took the opportunity to fill her in, without taking his eyes from the road. 'As you're probably aware, the old bothy's been standing unused for years. I've had it partially rebuilt, and electricity and plumbing put in—though, as a back-up system in case of power cuts, it's also equipped with Calor gas.' He paused to smoothly negotiate a tricky hairpin bend. 'It'll sleep eight comfortably, but more than twice that number in an emergency. It's in an ideal spot for climbers setting out to conquer Ben a-Coih—to refresh themselves and prepare for the climb ahead. Or, if the weather turns bad, it's a good place to hole up until it clears.'

It sounded like an excellent idea, but she couldn't resist the urge to pick holes. 'How can you be sure it'll only be used by *bona fide* mountaineers?'

A smile flickered across his lips. 'It's not exactly in a position where anyone other than climbers is likely to be passing by. I doubt we'll be bothered by squatters, if that's what you mean.'

'Very funny! I didn't mean that.' As he was perfectly aware. 'But it could be used by climbers other than from the centre,' she reasoned. 'And I'm sure you wouldn't want the riff-raff using it for free.'

He frowned and changed into a lower gear as the gradient increased. 'There'll be a system of keys,' he informed her as the engine revved. 'Anyone who's likely to be using the bothy will be given a key

before they set out. Although,' he added, flicking her
a glance, 'our doors will naturally not be closed to
other, independent climbers who need a roof over
their heads.'

'For a fee, no doubt.'

'Naturally, for a fee. Except in cases of emergency.'

'And who decides what's an emergency?'

'The climbers themselves. I reckon they're the best
judges of that.'

'How liberal!'

'No, merely practical. It's a system that works
without any hassles back home, as I'm sure it will
here as well. Activities like climbing,' he informed
her on a lightly condescending note, 'where a man
has to rely, sometimes for his life, on the reliability of
his companions, tend to bring out the best in people.
It's like a fraternity. When you're hanging two
hundred feet over a rock-face, you've got to be one
hundred per cent sure that you can trust the guy on
the end of the rope.'

'A noble brotherhood,' she responded, scoffing,
though she suspected it was probably true—and that
Brett knew from first-hand experience precisely what
he was talking about. He would be a man's man at
heart, with a love of adventure in his soul—and
respected by his peers as such. She turned away to
gaze out at the heavy sky. 'These people we're going
to see,' she said. 'Tell me who they are.'

'Angus and Janet MacKinnon, by name. It'll be
their job to run the place. To make sure there's a
constant supply of Calor gas and plenty of cans of
food on the shelves. Clean blankets and sheets, first-
aid equipment, all that kind of thing. In his younger

day, Angus used to be a mountain guide, so he can supply advice as well, and Janet runs a tiny store that serves the local farms and crofts, so she knows all about that side of things.' As a sudden flurry of snow swept the windscreen, he turned with a brief smile to look at her. 'I know we don't often agree, but I think you'll be quite impressed by them.'

She was. She liked them both enormously the minute she set eyes on them. He was a thin, wiry man with a face as grooved as a hunk of rock, she a red-cheeked, smiling matron with a floral pinny and a neat brown bun. They were waiting in the bothy with a pot of delicious-smelling coffee brewing on the stove. 'So, this is the young lady from the newspaper,' Janet beamed at Sarah after greeting Brett with a warm handshake. 'Come in, lass. Have a cup of coffee and warm yourself by the fire.'

It all went off more like an informal chat than an interview—and for once Brett kept very much to the background, seating himself in a corner with a mug of coffee and assuring Sarah with a wink, 'Carry on. This is your show. I'm just the chauffeur, remember?'

It was really the MacKinnons' show. There was something quite touching about the pride in their eyes as they showed Sarah round, pointing out every detail of the smartly fitted bathroom, tiny kitchenette and main room with its carpeted floor and comfortable-looking bunk beds.

'Such luxury!' Janet giggled delightedly as Sarah took some photographs. 'I tell you, our local lads have never seen the like of this!'

Afterwards, the MacKinnons invited Brett and

Sarah to go on to their place for lunch. And, though
Brett would rather have gone straight back, on a nod
from Sarah, he agreed in the end.

'You couldn't say no,' Sarah confided to him as
they set off in convoy for the tiny, isolated crofter's
cottage a few miles farther up the road. 'Janet
obviously has something special prepared.'

She was right. The delicious spread that awaited
them was most assuredly not everyday crofter's fare.
As they filed into the tiny dining-room, Brett threw
her a grateful wink, and Sarah found herself smiling
back at him with reciprocal gratitude of her own. The
gesture meant a lot to the MacKinnons, she could tell.
They would have been sorely disappointed if Brett
had insisted on going straight back.

To Janet's obvious further delight, he followed her
through to the kitchen while Angus sat down at the
table and Sarah laid out the plates and things.

'If you ask me, that lad's the best thing that's
happened to the area since they first brought in the
electricity,' Angus confided, *sotto voce*. 'He's given us
all a new lease of life.'

Sarah nodded politely as she arranged a napkin at
each place. 'He's certainly made some changes,' she
assented non-committally.

'Our two oldest sons have both got jobs at the
centre,' Angus went on. 'As sports instructors, no
less,' he added with pride. 'And we would have lost
them, if it hadn't been for Mr McCabe. They were
both on the point of leaving the Highlands and going
down south to look for jobs.'

With genuinely mixed feelings, Sarah glanced up at
the dark-haired man who appeared in the kitchen

doorway just then, carrying aloft a tureen of Scotch broth and grinning almost as widely as the red-cheeked woman at his side. If only all the things that everyone believed about him were true: that he really was some kind of saviour who could permanently transform their lives and give places like Cairn Ban and Strathbiggin a second chance. No one would support him more wholeheartedly than she.

The mood was light and informally congenial as they settled round the scrubbed pine table. And as she watched him chat and joke with his hosts, Sarah found herself reflecting that at least no one could accuse Brett of assuming airs. The self-made, multi-millionaire landowner was undoubtedly accustomed to moving in far more exalted circles these days, but he hadn't lost the common touch.

After a substantial second helping of rabbit stew, he pushed back his plate. 'That was terrific,' he told Janet. 'If I'd known what good cooks you Highland women are——' he flicked a glance to include Sarah in the remark '—I'd have made the transatlantic journey a long time ago.'

Janet glowed at the compliment and threw an appraising look at her auburn-haired guest. 'Does the young lady cook as well?' she enquired curiously.

'Like a dream,' Brett assured her, wicked amusement dancing in his eyes as Sarah flushed slightly and regarded him wryly over her plate.

'She's certainly a clever lass,' Janet observed, adding to Sarah's embarrassment, 'what with all that writing she does for the newspaper.'

'A girl of many talents—as I keep telling her.'

Sarah resisted the urge to kick him under the table,

and instead offered conclusive proof that she was, after all, capable of accepting compliments gracefully when she put her mind to it. 'We Highland women are renowned for our many talents,' she assured him with a smile. Then added as he smiled back at her approvingly, 'And for our natural Highland spirit. There's nothing and no one that can conquer us if we're really determined to put up a fight.'

He raised an eyebrow at her. 'Nothing?'

'And no one.' She held his gaze.

Then Angus cut in. 'Aye, they're a tough breed,' he acknowledged, slipping an arm affectionately round his wife's shoulder. Then added to Sarah's slight discomfort, as Brett continued to hold her eyes, 'But, believe me, there are no women in the world who can make a man happier.'

They ended up staying a little too long. It was well after three when the blue Range Rover drew away from the little stone cottage at last and set off back down the steep, winding road. It had been snowing on and off for the past couple of hours. Thin, undecided little flurries that might not come to anything. But, about five miles down the road, the sky turned ominously black and Brett cursed harshly under his breath. 'I knew we shouldn't have hung around. We're in for a deluge now.'

He hunched over the wheel and frowned, slowing their speed to an ultra-cautious few miles an hour as the car's wipers made an ever-increasingly futile attempt to cope with the sudden downpour. All at once, there was nothing to see all round but a swirling mass of snow.

It was like a solid, dancing wall, thick and

impenetrable, confusing and dazzling at the same time, cutting them off from the rest of the world. In a matter of seconds, visibility had been cut to under a yard, slowing their progress even more. And the blizzard was thickening all the time. It seemed to be closing in on them.

On a sudden wave of claustrophobia, Sarah tensed slightly in her seat. Thank God it was Brett at her side, she thought, and glanced warily across at him.

The dark brow was furrowed in concentration as he inched the car forward, battling against the advancing tide. But, eventually, he admitted defeat. 'Damn.' Swearing volubly, he pulled on the brake, then abruptly commanded as he reached for the door, 'You stay here. I want to try and check where we are. I don't even know if we're still on the road.'

The next moment, the door slammed behind him, and, with an abruptness that made Sarah shiver, he was swallowed up in the swirling snow. 'Dear Lord,' she found herself praying beneath her breath, 'please don't let him get lost.' And almost smiled at the bitter irony of the sentiment. Who would ever have believed she'd be praying for Brett McCabe's safe return?

And he was gone for far too long. As she sat there in the semi-gloom, listening to the throb of the engine and watching the snowflakes get bigger and thicker, mild claustrophobia turned to panic. What if he really had lost his way? It was possible, after all. Fear clutched at her throat at the thought of being stranded here on her own. Without him, she'd never find her way home again.

She grabbed at the door-handle in sudden terror

and almost fell out of the car in her haste, feeling her boots sink up past her ankles in the soft, deep, snowy wilderness.

'Brett!' she called out into darkness. 'Brett, are you there?'

The flakes were spinning around her head, dizzying in their effect. It would be so easy to lose one's way, and already he could have gone quite far. She stumbled forward, searching for footprints, but finding none. Already, the blizzard had covered his tracks. It was as though he'd vanished off the face of the earth.

'Brett! Can you hear me?' she called again. But her voice hung frozen in the frosty air, carrying no distance at all. Her fear growing now with every breath, she stumbled on anxiously.

'What the hell do you think you're doing?' She gasped as a strong hand suddenly reached out and grabbed her roughly by the arm. Then a shadowy figure loomed out of the darkness and he was right there, scowling down at her. 'I thought I told you to stay in the car!'

'I thought you were lost!' Relief in the form of a stupid grin spread helplessly across her face. She could have wept. She could have kissed him. She'd never felt so happy to see anyone in her life.

He didn't appear to share her joy. 'Well, I wasn't lost!' he rasped. 'But I very well might have been if I'd ended up having to search for you!' He propelled her unceremoniously back to the car and lifted her bodily inside. 'Let's get one thing absolutely straight,' he told her in a blistering voice. 'In this situation, I'm in charge!'

So, what's new? Sarah thought. Though she wouldn't have dared say it out loud. She could see, reluctantly, that he was right. In a moment of total, thoughtless panic, she'd endangered both their lives.

He climbed in beside her and switched the car's engine off. 'It's nothing less than a bloody nightmare out there. I reckon we'd be out of our minds even to think of carrying on.' The wide mouth firmed in a grim, straight line. 'One badly calculated bend and we could end up plunging over the edge.'

The snowflakes that had been clinging to his hair, in the heat of the car, had started to melt. Little beads of water, glistening like jewels. She looked away. 'So, what are we going to do?' she asked.

'There's not a lot we can do. We're stuck, I'm afraid.' He struck the steering wheel impatiently with the heel of his hand, then swivelled round to look at her. 'However, rather than stay here and risk dying of hypothermia, we could try and make it back to the bothy on foot. If I'm right, it's less than half a mile back along the road.'

'Are you sure?' How he could possibly know that was a total mystery to Sarah. She'd lost her bearings miles ago.

'Ninety per cent.' He smiled a faintly self-mocking smile. 'If you're prepared to trust me, we'll take a chance. If not, we'll stay here in the car.' He raised an eyebrow in challenge at her. 'I leave the decision up to you.'

It was some decision, and it reminded her of what he'd been saying earlier. In matters of life and death, you needed to be sure beyond a shred of doubt that you could trust the guy on the end of the rope. In the course of day-to-day events, she wouldn't trust him a single inch, but some instinct told her that, in a crisis like this, she could trust him totally. She nodded, her decision made. 'Let's try and get back to the bothy,' she said.

'Good girl.' He smiled and winked at her. Then, instantly, his expression became serious again. 'Just remember, I'm in charge. You do what I say, you follow me and you don't go wandering off on your own.'

There was absolutely no fear of that. She intended sticking to him like glue. But all the same she bristled a bit. 'I'm not an idiot, you know.'

'Let's hope not. For both our sakes.' He reached quickly into the back seat and grabbed a small haversack. 'It's a survival pack,' he informed her, slipping a compass from one of its pockets before slinging the bag across his back. Then added as she blanched a bit, 'Here's your chance to show a bit of that Highland spirit you were talking about.'

Indeed! As he set off ahead of her, long legs striding with comparative ease through the thigh-high drifts, she jammed her green tam-o'-shanter on her head and hurried determinedly after him. Less than half a mile, he'd said. At this rate, it would take them at least an hour.

After less than fifteen minutes, her legs felt as though they might drop off. Her body was aching from shoulder to thigh from the effort of keeping up with him. After half an hour, she had a searing pain in her side and she was literally gasping for breath. But she knew better than to beg him to stop and rest. This was no time for weak and womanish whimpering. If the effort brought her to her knees, she would prove herself as tough and reliable a teammate as Brett McCabe had ever had.

The bothy appeared before them at last, like some magnificent mirage.

'Congratulations!' As a tide of relief swept exhaustion away, she felt generous enough for a word of praise. Not many people, even trained mountaineers, could navigate through conditions like that. Then she added wryly, in case the praise should go to his head, 'Now let's hope you've got a key.'

'What key?' He brushed the snowflakes from his hair and feigned a look of blank surprise. 'I was rather relying on you to break in through the window,' he smiled.

'How very humorous.' She parodied a smile. Though she was relieved to see it was indeed a joke as the door swung open and he stepped aside.

The she lowered her eyes abruptly as he informed her quietly, 'You did very well. I know now that Angus was right about one thing, at least.'

Inside, there was a lingering warmth from the fire that had been burning earlier. Sarah could feel her cheeks start to tingle as her frozen nerve-ends came back to life. She pulled off her woollen beret, caked with snow, and shook out her damp auburn hair; blew against her frozen fingers and stamped the wet snow from her boots. Her entire body felt numb with weariness and cold.

Brett crossed over to the Calor gas stove and quickly switched it on. 'This should have the place heated up in no time at all.' Then he unzipped the heavy blue anorak and started to peel off his boots.

'I'll rustle up some coffee while you get into a nice hot bath.'

Sarah frowned at him, failing to comprehend. Hot baths and cups of coffee were the last things on her mind. 'I'd rather you just got on the phone and got someone to get us out of here.'

'And how do you reckon they're going to do that? On a magic carpet, perhaps?' He tossed the wet boots into a corner with a dismissive sigh. 'No, Sarah, we're stranded here, I'm afraid. We can't get out and no one can get in—at least, not tonight. By tomorrow morning, with any luck, the snowploughs will have cleared a path.'

'Tomorrow morning?' As the implication of what he was saying gradually sank in, the relief she'd felt a moment ago suddenly started to ebb away. 'Do you mean we have to sleep here?' she croaked. And it was the 'we' that stuck in her throat. It had never even occurred to her that they might have to spend the night together.

He was smiling as he filled the kettle and laid it on the stove, evidently amused at the consternation on her face. 'Don't worry, there are plenty of beds.' He lit a match and gestured airily round the room. 'We don't have to share if you'd rather not.'

'I don't find that funny in the least.' She folded her arms across her chest. 'Maybe you don't mind sleeping with strangers, but I'm afraid I do.' It was not at all what she'd intended to say, and in bleak embarrassment she bit her lip. 'I'm sorry, we'll have to find other arrangements,' she amended hurriedly.

He shrugged indifferently and lit the flame. 'Suit yourself,' he said. 'You can go back to the car, if you like, but I'm definitely staying here.' He turned with galling composure to cast an amused blue eye at her. 'Right now, I suggest you get undressed and think it over in the bath.'

There was nothing to think over, of course. She knew that as well as he. But she cast him a warning glance as she stalked past him to the bathroom door. 'Just so you know how I feel,' she bit back. 'I don't care for this arrangement at all.'

To add even further to her dismay, there was no lock on the bathroom door. 'Men don't bother about things like that,' he told her when she complained.

'Well, women do, so kindly don't come barging in!'

He threw her a disdainful smile. 'I'll do my best to control myself.' Then added as she slammed the door, 'Throw out your wet things before you get in and I'll dry them in front of the fire.'

She did as he said, then plunged with acute relief into the steaming bath. There were no bubbles, of course—men didn't bother about such things!—but as the warmth enveloped her stiff, chilled limbs it felt like sheer heaven, all the same. She leaned back with a sigh and closed her eyes, letting her body and mind relax, feeling the raw ache in her legs melt away and her inner tensions subside.

And, all at once, it dawned on her how childish she'd been to make a fuss. The hard truth of the matter was, she was lucky to be alive.

She could have lain there quite happily for an hour—but Brett was probably just as much in need of a relaxing bath as she. So, reluctantly, after a luxuriously soothing fifteen minutes, she climbed out and grabbed a towel from the pile on the stool at the end of the bath, feeling the stimulating roughness of the fresh-scented cotton against her skin as, hurriedly, she rubbed herself down. No thick, fluffy, effeminate towels here! This place was definitely geared for men!

It was then that she realised she had no clothes. Clutching the damp towel around her breasts, she opened the door a crack and, with all the delicacy of a nun, poked her head outside. 'I'm finished now!' she called. 'Can you hand me back my things?'

In answer, he stood up and started to come towards her across the room. 'They're not dry yet, I'm afraid.'

In alarm, she darted back. 'What the——!'

But he was far too fast for her. Before she could retreat all the way, he was right there in front of her, thrusting what appeared to be a crisp white folded bedsheet into her arms. 'Wrap this around you instead,' he instructed with a light, amused smile. Then stepped back abruptly and closed the door.

She felt like a cross between Mahatma Gandhi and a citizen of Ancient Rome when she finally emerged, with at least her modesty well guarded beneath the voluminous folds. She had draped one corner of the sheet across her shoulder, in an effort at style, and swathed the rest around her waist, in the interests of security. And she couldn't quite suppress an answering smile at the amused expression on his face. 'What the well-dressed journalist is wearing this winter,' she informed him with a giggle, and did a little twirl.

'Most engaging,' he approved, following her with his eyes as she crossed to stand in front of the fire. Then he pointed to the mug of coffee standing on the table nearby. 'While you're drinking that, have a rummage around in the cupboards and see what there is to eat. In spite of that enormous lunch we had, I'll be ready to eat in a little while.' Then, clutching a mug of coffee and a sheet of his own, he disappeared into the steam-filled bathroom.

Sarah made a couple of phone calls first. To McAndrew, to explain what had happened, and then to Uncle Dougal. The old man sounded greatly relieved. 'I was fair worried when I heard about that freak snowstorm up there. But I'll rest easy now that I know you're safe with Brett.'

She smiled faintly as she laid the phone down. There was something vaguely irritating about the way the entire world constantly kept expressing such confidence in the man. As though he were infallible. She sniffed—yet she was undeniably aware that she shared some of that confidence, too. Back there in the blizzard, the only moment of fear she'd known was when he had disappeared. Perhaps it was rash—and presumptuous, too—but, as long as he was with her, she'd known she'd be safe.

She drank the coffee, savouring its bitter warmth, then crossed to the food cupboard in the little kitchenette and peered curiously inside. Like him, in spite of their substantial lunch, she was starting to feel peckish again. It must be all the excitement, she thought. There was nothing like a bit of drama for burning up the calories.

There was no shortage of replacement calories

stacked on the shelves. Countless cans of ravioli, rice pudding and mushroom soup. What her Uncle Dougal would call cold-weather food—the sort of fare that sticks to your ribs. And to your waistline! she reminded herself, and diligently poked around for something else.

And then she spotted them, tucked at the back. A pile of packets of Indian curry—korma, biryani and vindaloo. She smiled to herself as she lifted them down. Considering the nature of her garb, the solution seemed highly appropriate. Happily, she bent to search around for pots and pans—and, as though in vocal and approval of this move, a deep tuneful baritone suddenly burst into song on the other side of the bathroom door.

She was stirring the vindaloo when he made her jump.

'Hey, that smells terrific!'

He was standing in the bathroom doorway, with the sheet wrapped round his waist, the strong, tanned torso naked and exposed. And, impulsively, at the sight of him Sarah felt her stomach contract. Dressed, he was already quite striking enough; half-naked, he was a feast for the eyes.

Abruptly, she turned back to stirring the vindaloo. 'It'll be ready in about twenty minutes,' she said.

Outside, the snow had finally stopped, but as Sarah pulled the curtains closed, the sky was already as black as night. As she turned around to fetch the dishes of curry from the kitchenette, he was scattering pillows from the bunk beds on to the floor in front of the fire.

'Much cosier than sitting at the table, don't you think?' he suggested as she frowned.

She shrugged. 'I suppose so.' She had to agree. The little square table in the corner with its hard-backed, functional-looking chairs didn't look cosy in the least. It was just that she had a lingering doubt about how cosy she wanted to be.

The meal turned out surprisingly good—and the couple of cans of beer that Brett had dug out from the back of the cupboard helped very pleasantly to wash it down. Perhaps out of deference to her blushes, he had donned his now dry shirt, though it hung loosely open at the front and he had rolled back the sleeves.

Whatever the reason, Sarah, for once, felt quite at ease. Perhaps it was the sheer absurdity of the situation, she wondered to herself, or the fact that they'd been thrown together in a jam. For there was none of the usual spiked antagonism in the air. None of the biting sarcasm. No trace of antipathy. Unlikely as it seemed, the two of them were laughing and chattering together almost as though they were old friends.

As they pushed aside the empty plates and lolled back against the piled-up pillows, she smiled across at him and joked, 'All we need now is a big bowl of fruit, then we could lounge around like Ancient Romans and peel each other grapes.'

He looked at her curiously for a moment, then inclined his dark head as he enquired, 'Beneath that Calvinistic exterior, do I detect a hint of decadence?'

'Perhaps.' Her eyes held his, though it might have

been wise to look away. 'In spite of my heritage, I've nothing against the occasional excess.'

'I'm glad to hear it.' His gaze scanned her face. 'I subscribe to a similar philisophy myself.'

He was half sitting, half lying with his arms stretched out along the pillows, and she could see quite clearly from the corner of her eye the line of fine black hairs that ran from sun-burnished elbow to strong, supple wrist. As he straightened and leaned a little towards her now, she made no attempt to move, though the tips of his fingers touching her arm were like a jolt of electricity.

'I knew we were bound to find something in common eventually.' He was smiling a gentle smile, though it wasn't humour shining from his eyes. A fierce intensity that she had never glimpsed before was burning in their depths.

As his fingers moved to touch her shoulder, Sarah held her breath, feeling the hectic beat of her heart as her eyes fixed helplessly on his face. And she seemed to drown in the pools of his eyes as, soft as a feather now, his hand slid beneath the protective folds to touch the sensitive skin of her throat.

The world had gone completely still. No movement in time or space. As his hand moved downwards, his touch like fire, she suddenly felt her stomach clench. A throb of excitement tore at her soul as he paused to caress the swell of her breast, his fingers lingering and firm as they grazed the stiff, hard peak.

But he had only just begun his tantalising work. With a shudder, Sarah leaned back, at the mercy of the longing that pulsed through her veins, and, dry-

mouthed, closed her eyes as, slowly and with the
utmost delicacy, he began to peel away the
sheet . . .

CHAPTER SIX

SARAH lay very still, staring up into the night, watching the glow from the Calor gas fire throw strange, dark shadows on to the wall. Outside, the wind had ceased its moaning at last and the only sounds to reach her ears were the slow, peaceful rhythm of Brett's breathing from across the room and the contrasting frantic tempo of her own still wildly beating heart.

She sighed and smiled a bitter smile and turned over restlessly to face the wall. She'd been tossing and turning for hours now while, gallingly, he slept like a child. And, though she closed her eyes and breathed slowly, the oblivion she craved refused to come. There were too many unquiet images dancing like demons across her brain.

She pulled the covers over her head and curled into a small tight ball. What had passed between them earlier had evidently left him quite unmoved—though there had definitely been no disguising his lack of indifference at the time—but it had left Sarah confused and shaken and still struggling to come to terms with it.

It could not have happened, she kept telling herself. She had never let go like that before. But her still-tingling nerve-ends and sensitised flesh dictated a reality of their own. Whether her mind cared to accommodate the fact or not, her body was only too well aware of its bittersweet, sensual awakening.

And that was why she couldn't sleep. Why she'd spent the last two tortured hours reliving over and over again each cruelly delicious moment of it.

As he'd started to slip the sheet from her shoulder, she'd felt her heart skip an anxious beat, and an odd mix of panic and excitement had made her breath catch in her throat. And she should have made some protest then to stop the madness going ahead, but all at once she'd been incapable of articulating a single word. Instead, she gasped soundlessly and closed her eyes as she felt him slide across the cushions with a sigh and draw her softly into his arms.

'Sarah, Sarah, my lovely.' He breathed her name against her face as his hands caressed her shoulders and neck, and never had the touch of any man felt so overpoweringly sweet.

With a moan, she let her head drop back as she felt his lips move to her throat. Then shuddered as, in one swift, urgent movement, his hand swept down to peel away the folds of the sheet from her naked breasts.

'Sarah, let me look at you. Let me see how beautiful you are.' He drew back for a moment to pay homage to her with his eyes, then reached out with a sigh of satisfaction to cup each firm, proud orb with his hand.

His touch was like fire against her flesh. Her mouth had suddenly gone dry. As his fingers moved in lazy, tantalising circles, he seemed to be deliberately driving her wild. Then, as though in answer to her unspoken plea, he bent down suddenly to draw into his mouth each throbbing, excited peak in turn.

A feeling of voluptuous pleasure surged through her as the heat of his lips tugged at her flesh. And she felt her back arch and her breathing grow ragged as his tongue strummed a silent, erotic tune.

She wanted him then with an intensity with which she had wanted nothing before in her life. With a wild, unreasoning, unfettered abandon that shook her to her very soul. On a reckless wave, she clung to him, fingers twining in the thick, dark hair, reaching to caress with hungry wonder the hard, supple contours of his shoulders and chest.

Nothing like this had ever happened to her. She could scarcely believe it was happening now.

In a movement, he had shed his shirt and tossed it impatiently to one side. Then he gazed down at her with burning blue eyes as he smoothed the auburn hair from her face.

'Sarah, Sarah, my sweet.' As he kissed her chin, her cheek, her ear, sending shivers of excitement racing through her blood, she pressed her face against his neck, devouring the heady, male scent of him. Feeling her teeth graze the warm, taut skin as she buried her lips in urgent response.

Gently now, he lowered himself on top of her, the lightly abrasive brush of his chest against her eager, upturned breasts triggering unexpected shock-waves of delight. And, low down, an aching throb awakened as she felt through the flimsy barrier of the sheets the urgent, thrusting manifestation of his own unsated male desire. As his hands reached down to mould her hips, she longed to cry out his name, but dared utter no more than a strangled moan as his mouth came down at last to claim fierce possession of her own.

It was like the bursting of a dam to feel the power of passion in him—and to experience the instinctive echo of her own body's heated, abandoned response. As he eased her aching lips apart, invading her with his tongue, she tautened herself against him, unashamedly begging for more.

Yet, a moment later, as she felt his hand glide downwards to finally free the sheet at her waist, a sudden, belated sense of apprehension started to creep over her. Involuntarily, she froze. She was, after all, on the brink of taking a step that she had never taken before. This was the farthest along the path of love that she had come with any man.

He instantly picked up the change in her and paused with a question in his eyes. Then he breathed in sharply and slid away before she could say a word. His voice was husky, deep in his throat. 'I think we'd better stop here,' he said.

It was as though a barrier had dropped, closing him in and shutting her out. With a hasty adjustment of the sheet at his waist, abruptly he started to get to his feet. 'I think we should get some sleep now,' he told her. 'I'd like to make an early start.'

For a moment, Sarah didn't move. She felt bewildered, slightly shocked, her bearings totally at sea, as though she'd been dropped from an enormous height. She blinked at the tall, dark figure, suddenly so detached and remote, the white-hot heat that had blazed in his eyes doused now to unnerving ice.

'That would suit me very well,' she managed in a croaky voice and, grabbing at her shattered dignity, snatched the discarded sheet to her breast.

Of course, she should have felt grateful to him. She was aware of that. Grateful and deeply relieved that his control had stopped them both in time. But, as she'd watched him turn away—and, even now, as she lay sleepless in the dark—a sense of relief and gratitude were not among the emotions she felt.

Instead, through the still-pounding pulses of her rudely awakened heart, she felt a shaft of disappointment, even regret. A man's man he may be, she thought with chagrin, but Brett McCabe was much more than that. He was the lover who, if only she'd dared, could at last have awakened her woman's soul.

Through sheer, irresistible exhaustion, Sarah did finally fall asleep. But it was an uneasy, fitful sleep, plagued by vivid, disturbing dreams. It was almost a relief when she awoke with a jolt to discover that morning had arrived.

Without moving, she could see that Brett's bed was empty, and she could hear the sounds of splashing water coming from the bathroom next door. She pulled one arm from the bedclothes and glanced quickly at her watch. Six-thirty. She frowned. He hadn't been joking about that early start.

As the bathroom door opened, she held her breath and pretended still to be asleep, but watched curiously through slitted eyes as he stalked silently across the room.

He was dressed only in his jeans, with a white towel slung around his neck, a shadow of dark beard at his chin, the black hair brushed back from his face. And as he crossed to the bunk where he had slept and bent down quickly to pull on his boots, Sarah was suddenly uncomfortably aware that her heart was pumping like a piston in her chest.

Then something quickened inside her, deep and instant as a flash of pain, as the broad back straightened suddenly and the muscles of his shoulders flexed. For one vivid instant, she knew again the powerful, giddy pull of his flesh, the vibrant feel of those hard, male contours moving beneath her fingertips.

She snapped her eyes shut and swallowed hard, giving herself a mental shake. Last night had been an error of judgement. They had caught each other unawares. The threatening, unnatural circumstances and the shared sense of relief had somehow contrived to create a bond that was totally and treacherously false. It was crazy, but it was hardly surprising that they'd fallen into each other's arms.

Now, in the sober light of day, she must face up to her mistake. Put it behind her, as he surely would, and never let it happen again.

With hastily gathered detachment, Sarah reopened her eyes, grateful to see that he'd pulled on his shirt and was tucking it into the waist of his jeans. Next came the red pullover and the heavy blue anorak, zipped to the neck. So, he was going out. That was good. It would give her a chance to gather herself.

A moment or two later, with a rush of cold wind, he pulled the bothy door open, stepped outside, then quickly closed it again. Sarah waited until she was sure he was gone, then with a sigh she climbed out of bed.

She had slept in her sweater and trousers, unwilling to risk a state of undress, and after all those hours of tossing and turning she felt decidedly crumpled now. She went through to the bathroom and had a good wash, brushed her teeth with her fingers and tidied her hair. However uneasy she might really feel, at least on the outside she should appear composed. He would be, she reminded herself, as, marginally satisfied, she went back through to the main room and pulled the heavy curtains wide.

In spite of the early hour, it was already light. And, though yesterday's blizzard had finally stopped, its icy breath had transformed the land. As far as the eye could see, the universe was white. A vast expanse of snowscape, barren as the moon, its surface rippled with frosty peaks, like some gigantic meringue. And the only sign that life existed somewhere in this desert of ice was a set of pitted footsteps leading down towards the road.

Brett's footsteps. With a sharp sigh, Sarah turned away. What would suit her most of all was if those footsteps were heading right out of her life.

She was cooking a can of sausages and beans, and there was a pot of coffee bubbling on the stove, when, half an hour or so later, she heard the Range Rover growl outside. A moment passed, then, with a stamping of feet, Brett opened the door. But she deliberately refrained from turning round as he stepped inside.

'So, you're up.' He sounded neither surprised nor pleased. It was a simple, impersonal statement of fact.

Sarah kept her eyes fixed on the pan and gave the sausages another stir, all at once oddly uncertain of how she should react to him. 'I hear you got the car back,' she replied.

She heard him unzip the heavy blue anorak and toss it casually on to a chair, then come slowly across the room to stand just a few feet away. 'The road's still pretty bad, but I've put the snow chains on. Now that it's light, we should have no great difficulty getting back.'

'That's a relief.' She stirred some more, then informed him over her shoulder, 'I'm making some breakfast, by the way.'

He shot her a cool look. 'Then I suggest we get on with it quickly. I'd rather not waste unnecessary time.'

Quite involuntarily, she winced. There was something about the way he'd said it, as though he was issuing a command, that was faintly shocking, even hurtful. She whirled round defensively. 'Don't worry, I'm just as anxious as you are to get out of here! I couldn't bear to be stuck in this place a moment longer than necessary!'

He was standing with his thumbs hooked loosely in the pockets of his jeans, regarding her through narrowed lids, his expression unfathomable. And there was something faintly sinister about the dark, unshaven jaw. 'Well, you won't be,' he guaranteed her with a sardonic smile. 'Not one moment longer than necessary. So you can relax.'

She glared at him. She's been relaxed enough until he'd appeared, but now her stomach had started to churn.

He turned away. 'The journey should take us a couple of hours. Less, if we're lucky and snow ploughs have been out.' He paused and glanced down at his watch, then tossed her a condescending smile. 'Carry on with your cooking. An extra half-hour or so won't make a great deal of difference.'

Arrogant swine! A rush of resentment swept through her as he turned away. How dared he treat her as though she were some serving girl? Trembling, she tipped a heap of sausages and beans on to a couple of plates and informed him over her shoulder, lacing each word with spite, 'If you don't mind, I'd prefer to eat at the table this time. I haven't the slightest desire for a repetition of last night.'

It was the sort of nakedly loaded comment that might have been better left unsaid, but she was suddenly overcome by a compulsive need to lash out at him. The trouble was, as she knew too well, he was perfectly liable to lash right back. As a hot light flashed in his eyes, she felt her heart give an uneasy lurch.

But nothing in the world could have prepared her for his response.

'I'm sorry about last night,' he said. 'It should never have happened. I apologise.'

It was the last thing she'd ever expected to hear, and it took a moment for the words to sink in. Some cutting slander about how she'd led him on, some mocking allusion to her own loss of control—that was the order of response she'd expected him to come back at her with. Instead, this dignified apology took her totally by surprise. She stared at him blankly as he went on, 'We'll forget it ever happened. I think that's best.'

Without looking at him, she picked up the plates and crossed to the table. 'I accept your apology,' she said. 'The whole thing never happened, as far as I'm concerned.'

Barely a word was spoken over the sausages and beans, and barely the flicker of a glance exchanged. And it seemed as though the gulf between them was wider now that it had ever been, the two friends and almost-lovers of the night before mysteriously vanished without a trace. All that remained were two awkward strangers, natural enemies once again.

They encountered no particular problems on the way down, and, as Brett had optimistically predicted, the snow ploughs were already out. In less than an hour they'd left the most treacherous stretch of mountain road behind, the tarmac widening and straightening out of its corkscrew curves as they came in sight at last of Loch Coih.

Yet, as they headed homewards round the glen, Sarah's mood was not as jubilant as it ought to have been. She felt oddly deflated, emotionally flat—with an uncomfortable, prickly awareness of the remote, silent figure at her side.

The first part was hardly surprising, she hurried to assure herself. A natural sense of anticlimax after the hectic events of the past twenty-four hours. The rest was merely a hangover from the ill-advised intimacies of last night. The feeling would undoubtedly disappear the minute he was out of sight.

The Range Rover drew up outside the cottage just

after nine o'clock—with Sarah instantly scrambling for the door, apparently anxious to put her theory to the test.

'I'll see you around.' With a casual nod, he slammed the door shut. Then shifted into gear as she turned away.

Without a backward glance, she hurried down the path and heaved a sigh of relief as she reached the front door.

But, once in the safety of the darkened hall, she paused and turned her eyes back to the road. Then watched with a thinly victorious smile as he turned the car round and drove quickly away.

The relief that lit up Dougal's face a moment later when she walked in through the kitchen door was almost enough to bring tears to her eyes. He wrapped her in a bear-hug, as though she were a little child, his big heart beating in his chest.

'Lassie, I'm glad to see you,' he told her in a low, gruff voice. 'I hardly slept a wink all night.'

A fact which Mrs Campbell was quick to confirm as she poured them all a cup of tea. 'He was dozing in his armchair by the fire when I arrived this morning. He hadn't been to bed all night.'

Affectionately, Sarah squeezed his arm. 'It's good to be back where I belong.'

But the cosy reunion didn't last long. Just as she was thinking that she ought to call the paper and let McAndrew know she was safely back, the phone out in the hall began to ring. He had beaten her to it. And he had what he ominously described as 'a little job' for her.

'What is it?' she enquired, hoping against hope that it was nothing more demanding than a stuffy council meeting or a Boy Scouts' bazaar—just about all she felt capable of dealing with today. But she gasped in mingled shock and surprise as, in his usual downbeat manner, he enlightened her.

'There's been a fire. At the Baxters' place. I want you down there right away.'

'Bad?' she wondered aloud—and wondered privately why the news didn't fill her with more joy. On any other day but this, the image of the Baxters going up in flames would have brought an uncharitable smile to her face. But today, what struck her most forcefully was the sense of inevitability about the news. It seemed cruelly fitting, somehow, that the detested Baxters should crop up in the bitter wake of Brett McCabe.

McAndrew was answering her question. 'Bad enough, by all accounts, though no one's been injured, I understand. A *Gazette* photographer's been round and got us some damned good pictures of the blaze. What I want from you is an equally good story for the front page.'

So, it was in at the deep end! she thought. And promised, 'I'll get on to it right away.'

'Make sure you cover every angle.' Her boss paused before ending on a weighty note, 'There's been no confirmation yet, but there's talk of arson in the air.'

Arson? As Sarah took time for a quick shower and changed into fresh clothes before setting off, she mulled over the possibility in her mind. Her own initial explanation had been divine retribution, the wrath of God, but McAndrew's more prosaic suggestion definitely merited a second thought. There was no lack of people with grudges against the Baxters, after all. Half the local community would be happy to see them burnt to the ground.

Too bad. They would have to wait. As Sarah turned off the road into the driveway that led to the old baronial house, the sight that met her gaze was a disappointingly long way off from the smouldering heap of rubble and ashes that she'd been secretly hoping to see. The north-facing, ivy-covered façade showed no sign of damage at all. The only visible evidence that there'd been a fire at all was a thin plume of sooty smoke rising from the back of the house. If this was the work of some fire-raiser, he'd done a lamentably inefficient job.

She parked her little red Fiat under a clump of bare-branched trees, gathered up her notepad and strode to the door. 'I'm from the *Gazette*,' she informed the plump housekeeper who more or less instantly answered the bell. 'I've come to see Mr Baxter about the fire.'

'Come in. Wait here.' She was ushered inside, the door closed behind her and the woman vanished down the hall.

Sarah stuffed her hands into the pockets of her coat and glanced around her with a wary eye. The hall of the Baxter mansion was a massive place, designed, like the rest of the big, sprawling house, to intimidate and impress. Oak beams straddled the lofty ceiling from where hung suspended a huge chandelier, and well-worn Persian carpets adorned the highly-polished floor. Yet, in spite of its lavish proportions and undeniably grand décor, the house had always seemed to Sarah a peculiarly barren and empty place. Cold and somehow airless. As though it had no soul.

There was a sudden movement at the end of the hall as a burly, red-faced man appeared. 'Miss Drummond, I've been expecting you!' a loud, booming voice declared. 'Please join us, if you would be so good. My wife and I will see you now.'

Sarah hadn't even noticed the thin, gaunt female figure in brown, hovering self-effacingly in the shadow of the tweed-suited man. But then, that was perfectly normal, she reflected to herself as she followed them into a large, but faintly gloomy reception-room hung with paintings of local wildlife in heavy, ornately gilded frames. Mrs Baxter was renowned for her retiring ways. She was the timid and cringing antithesis of her bullying, bombastic spouse.

They all sat: Baxter, heavy legs spread in front of him, in one of the plush-upholstered armchairs; Sarah on the sofa opposite him, straight-backed and composed; and Mrs Baxter, like a guest in her own home, poised at her husband's shoulder on a hard-backed chair.

Baxter lost no time in coming straight to the point. 'You're here, of course, because of the fire.' He addressed himself to Sarah with a frown. 'A terrible, terrible business. The whole of the west wing in flames. The only thing we have to be grateful for is that nobody was hurt. If we hadn't raised the alarm when we did, it could have been a great deal worse.' He glanced in the direction of his wife with what Sarah suspected was a rare look of concern. 'My wife and my daughter and myself could have been burned to death in our beds.'

Somehow, it was not an image that brought instant tears to Sarah's eyes, but she managed to bestow a convincing smile of sympathy as she asked, 'I take it, then, that the west wing is the part of the house where the family sleeps?'

'Not so. Not so.' He shook his head. 'Our rooms are on the other side. The west wing comprises mainly guest-rooms and, luckily, none was occupied.'

'So, who was it who discovered the fire?'

'I did.' In an almost preening gesture, Baxter smoothed a palm across his thinning hair. 'It was about three o'clock and I couldn't sleep, so I went downstairs to make a cup of tea. And it was then that I smelt smoke. On investigation, I discovered that the west wing was ablaze and I immediately phoned the fire brigade.'

Sarah had opened her notepad and was jotting down a couple of things. How the devil looks after his own, she pondered wryly to herself. Trust Baxter to have insomnia on the very night someone tries to burn him down! Aloud, she asked him, 'How bad is the damage? What sort of estimate would you put on it?'

Thoughtfully, he rubbed his chin. 'Substantial,' he replied. 'Four rooms have been totally destroyed and the whole of the west wing made unsafe. I'm only taking a guess, of course—the official estimate has still to be made—but it will probably take hundreds of thousands of pounds to put the damage right.'

Substantial, by anyone's standards. 'I assume you were insured?'

'Oh, yes, thank God.' He smiled a smug smile. 'By a lucky chance, I took out an updated policy only a couple of months ago.'

Mentally, Sarah shook her head. It was a wholly unfair fact of life that, somehow, men like Baxter invariably seemed to land on their feet. In a deliberate attempt to cross him, she turned her attention to his wife. 'And what about you, Mrs Baxter? At the time your husband's talking about, were you aware of anything?'

The woman glanced at her husband, as though seeking permission to speak. 'I—eh——' she began. But before she could get any further, Baxter himself cut in.

'She was aware of nothing. She'd taken one of her sleeping pills.' There was unadorned contempt in his voice as the woman flushed and lowered her eyes. And Sarah found herself drawing a parallel with one of the wildlife scenes on the wall: a sleek and cold-eyed stoat with a lifeless fieldmouse in its jaws. No doubt, like Mrs Baxter, the mouse had died without a sound.

Sarah nodded. 'I see,' she said.

For good measure, Baxter assured her, 'A bomb could go off in the next room and she wouldn't know.'

'What's all this about a bomb? Wasn't the fire enough for you?' The door had opened and a slim, blonde figure dressed in blue was advancing graciously into the room. 'May I join you?' She smiled at her father and arranged herself on the arm of his chair, crossing the ankles of her soft kid boots and tossing back her long, fair hair.

For some reason, at the sight of her, Sarah felt her stomach clench. Unconsciously, she'd been hoping that Amanda wouldn't be at home.

Almost tangibly, the blonde girl's entrance had altered the chemistry in the room. Her mother, if that was possible, had retreated even further into her chair, while a milder, almost paternal look had stolen into the stoat-like eyes. 'Come, my dear,' he smiled at her. 'Come and help me with the Press.'

'Poor Father.' She brushed his arm with a solicitous hand and turned to his inquisitor with an appealing look. 'You must understand he's been answering questions since the first light of day. The police, the insurance people—and now you. You'll appreciate he's a little tired.'

She was inclined to be thin-faced, like her mother, but her cheeks bore the healthy bloom of youth. And with her stylish grooming and switched-on charm she could be quite striking when she wished. It was perfectly easy to understand why Brett had called her a good-looking girl.

The thought made Sarah defensive. 'I'm only doing my job,' she said.

'Oh, don't worry, we understand.' Amanda smoothed her skirt with a manicured hand. 'I'm sure all those silly questions must be just as tiresome for you.'

She was so immaculate, so composed, yet there was venom below that glossy veneer. Sarah bridled. 'Be that as it may,' she retorted, 'I still have a couple more silly questions to ask.' She pointedly switched her gaze back to Baxter. 'Have you any idea how the fire started? I understand there's some suspicion that it may have been deliberate.'

'*Suspicion?!*' Baxter was indignant. 'There's no doubt at all that it was a deliberate act of sabotage!'

'How do you know?'

'It was an act of revenge.' His face grew red. 'They deliberately tried to burn us down!'

'Who did? Why?' In spite of the man's wholly justifiable paranoia, she felt obliged to enlighten him. 'Most fires are accidents, you know. Ninety-nine-point-nine per cent. It could have been an electrical fault—have you considered the possibility of that?'

It was the wrong thing to say. 'It was no accident!' Baxter leaned forward belligerently in his chair, mean eyes flashing at her. 'And don't you throw statistics at me, young woman. I know what I'm talking about! I'm telling you it was deliberate—so don't you try and get clever with me!'

It was as though he'd slapped her. Sarah blanched. 'Now, just a minute!' she started to protest. But, before she could say another word, Amanda diplomatically cut in.

'My father's understandably very upset.' She urged forbearance with a honeyed smile. 'You see, we believe it was a former employee, Arthur Imrie, who was responsible.'

'Lazy, no-good bastard! I should have fired him years ago!'

She continued, ignoring the bad-tempered growls at her back, 'He was our game-keeper until a couple of months ago. But a troublemaker, I'm sorry to say.' She made a face, expressing distaste. 'My father had to let him go.'

A troublemaker, in the vocabulary of the Baxters, was someone who dared to stand up for his rights. Though she scarcely knew Arthur Imrie at all, Sarah was instantly on his side. She straightened in her seat and asked, 'What reason do you have for thinking it might have been him?'

Amanda made another face. 'You know what these people are like. They'd do anything for revenge. Besides,' she added, 'you must have heard. He threatened my father publicly.'

Sarah had heard. The public altercation between old man Baxter and his sacked gamekeeper was common knowledge in the town. She'd also heard reports that Imrie had been drinking at the time. She narrowed her eyes at Amanda, far from convinced. 'You can't accuse a man of something as serious as arson on the strength of something he said when he was drunk.'

'You can if you know he did it!' Baxter came to life again and glowered at her. 'Take my word for it, Miss Drummond, Imrie's a guilty man.'

'Do you have proof?'

'Not yet, but I'll get it. I intend to ruin that man.'

It was the first wrong move he'd made throughout the interview, but it was a fatally revealing one. Sarah leaned forward with a triumphant smile. Do you mind if I quote you on that?'

Amanda hurried to intervene. 'What my father means, of course, is that the truth will emerge. And that the due process of the law will punish the guilty for what has been done.' As her father started to open his mouth to make some blustering remark, she stretched out one arm and silenced him with a wave of her red-tipped hand. There was real steel behind that feminine façade, Sarah observed with a smile to herself. But the smile slid abruptly into oblivion as the blonde girl leaned towards her now.

'I'll tell you one thing you can quote, if you like.' Her eyes swept silkily over Sarah's face. 'The next one to suffer at the hands of the Imries will almost certainly be Brett McCabe.'

Hearing Brett's name on Amanda's lips, Sarah stiffened involuntarily. She swallowed. 'What do you mean?' she asked.

'Just this.' Amanda smoothed her creaseless skirt. 'He's been unwise enough to cross them, too. Just the other evening, when he was having dinner here, he happened to mention in passing that he'd turned Imrie's son down for a job. A key job, I understand, for which the boy wasn't qualified, of course—but apparently, in spite of that, he had the gall to make a fuss.' She made one of her disdainful faces and touched the gold chain at her throat. 'We thought nothing about it at the time, but now that this has happened . . .' She paused. 'Brett has to be warned. If these people *are* responsible for our fire, he could find himself in the same boat as us.'

What nonsense, thought Sarah. Nothing and nobody could harm Brett. Besides, maybe the Baxters had no shortage of enemies, but Brett was the most popular man in town!

So, it wasn't anxiety on his behalf that caused the sudden dull ache in her heart, nor her mouth all at once to feel like parchment as Amanda elaborated now, 'I'll talk to him this evening and warn him

myself—he's promised to drop round later and
commiserate with us over a drink.' She smiled an
almost coy smile and self-consciously shook back her
hair as she flicked a glance at her father, who nodded
dourly in support. Then, still smiling, she turned her
eyes once more to Sarah's ashen face. 'Now, is there
anything else, Miss Drummond, that you require to
know?'

There was nothing. Awkwardly, Sarah stood.
'Perhaps you could show me the damage now. I have
all the information I need.'

It was only a short walk along the snow-cleared
gravel pathway that completely encircled the old
house, the blonde girl in the mink coat out in front,
the redhead lagging a little behind. And it took only a
couple of minutes to inspect the gutted and
blackened west wing. Then a swift walk back to the
waiting car as Amanda hurried indoors again. But,
to Sarah, those few minutes felt like a tortured eternity.

With an unaccountably trembling hand, she
slammed the car door and switched on the engine.
How right she'd been in all her predictions regarding
the Baxters and Brett. And especially right, it would
appear, where Amanda was concerned.

He obviously hadn't wasted any time at all in
getting in touch with her. He must have phoned her
more or less the moment he got home.

She headed for the road. The accuracy of her
foresight was really quite uncanny. Everything she
had ever foretold was being made truth before her
eyes.

Yet, as she drove back along the empty, deserted

road, she felt no sense of triumph at the thought. Just an inexplicable sense of betrayal and a deep, unquenchable throb of grief.

CHAPTER SEVEN

SARAH was kept mercifully busy over the following couple of weeks. First, the weekend after the fire, Susie had her birthday party. And with Easter just around the corner, Strathbiggin was coming back to life.

There was a spate of seasonal receptions to cover, official openings and church bazaars—and a stream of musical and theatrical treats on offer at the local concert hall. And, to add to the general air of awakening, the snow had finally all but cleared. It was too early yet to talk of spring in these chilly northern latitudes, but its promise was definitely in the air.

Sarah was grateful for the sudden burst of activity. It helped to keep her mind off Brett. Not entirely, she had to admit, but at least for a few hours in every day.

The trouble was, he was a hard man to forget. Though he'd been keeping a diplomatic distance since the unfortunate bothy affair, she seemed destined to stumble across his shadow virtually everywhere she turned. Even now, mid-way through their morning coffee break, Tom had suddenly diverted her attention to an announcement on the front page of that morning's *Gazette*.

'Now there's a well-deserved honour,' he exclaimed. 'Old man Baxter's got it right for once!'

Politely, Sarah followed his pointing finger, though she already knew what he was talking about. Her Uncle Dougal, using almost exactly the same words, had shoved the announcement under her nose before she'd even started breakfast! She gave an elaborate, dismissive shrug. 'So, McCabe's to be guest of honour at the annual ceilidh? Big deal!' she scoffed.

Tom shot her a shrewd look. 'It may not exactly be dinner at Balmoral, but it's still one of the highest accolades that this town has to offer.'

She knew he was right. The annual shindig at the Baxters' mansion was a tradition that went back a hundred years: an evening of Highland song and dance when anyone who was anyone in the local community was invited to pass through the laird's hallowed doors. And 'guest of honour' was a title that had been parsimoniously bestowed in the past—granted only to a handful of deserving Lord Provosts and a couple of distinguished war heroes. Sarah's personal feelings aside, she knew well the honour that had been conceded to Brett.

With a cynical twist in her voice, she remarked, 'Baxter certainly got his timing right.'

And even Tom had to smile in agreemeent with that. 'It'll be a popular move with the town, all right.'

That was putting it mildly, thought Sarah as a call came through and Tom hurried away. Less than a week ago, as building finally commenced on the site, Brett had announced his intention to sponsor a local marathon. His standing, already high, had immediately gone straight through the roof. She shook her head with a bitter sigh. One might have expected old Baxter to rather resent the way he was being usurped—his days as top dog in the community were over, thanks to Brett. But you really had to hand it to him, he certainly knew how to roll with the tide.

What was more, the tide seemed to be rolling with him. According to evidence gathered at the fire, his allegations of arson had probably been right. A frightening thought that had even prompted a reluctant wave of sympathy from the locals. No one felt comfortable with the thought that there was an arsonist in their midst. And, though Sarah was as anxious as anyone that the culprits should be caught, she was privately pleased that, so far, at least, the Imries hadn't been implicated. They were a hot-headed bunch, by all accounts, but she had a feeling they weren't criminals. Besides, it would be galling in the extreme if Baxter was proved right about everything!

It was later that afternoon, on her return to the office from an outside job, that Tom passed on a message to her. 'McCabe's site manager called to ask if you could drop by later today. He's got something to show you, apparently.'

'He didn't say what?'

Tom shook his head. 'He wants you to see it for yourself.'

Sarah was curious. She glanced at her watch. 'In that case, I'll go now,' she said.

It wasn't Sarah's first visit to the site since that disastrous night on the mountain with Brett. Since the snow had cleared and the work had begun, she'd made several fleeting official visits. But always on the instructions of her boss, or in response, as now, to a summons from Ken. Brett himself had never been in touch with her again—a fact for which she was heartily glad. Nor had he made any further attempts to influence the reports she wrote. It seemed he'd finally relaxed his suffocating stranglehold.

As she turned into the castle road, she smiled a wry smile to herself. In spite of her sudden journalistic freedom, the tenor of her reports had changed little over the past couple of weeks. For the fact was—though she admitted it unwillingly—that she could find nothing unfavourable to write about the scheme. Perhaps, she was even beginning to wonder, all the pressure he had put on her initially had really been quite unnecessary.

As for the petition, she had shelved that for the time being. It had virtually died for lack of support. Though she herself was not entirely won over yet. His scheme might be sound, but what about the man himself? Could she really trust him yet?

The scene down on the site seemed to be changing before her eyes. Sarah blinked as she came round the back of the castle and drew up outside the site office. The vast expanse of long-neglected scrub that stretched down to Loch Coih had already been flattened and cleared by a pair of massive mechanical diggers. Concrete mixers were clanking, electric saws buzzing, while a team of giant cranes hoisted into place an intricate web of scaffolding.

Ken came hurrying to meet her as she climbed out of the car. 'Just look at this!' He waved an arm in the direction of all the furious activity and his ruddy face literally beamed with pride. 'This is what I call getting things done! We'll be finished the job well ahead of schedule if we keep going at this pace.'

Well, that was good news, Sarah told herself. The sooner the job was finished, the sooner Brett would be gone for good. She followed Ken round to the back of the site office to catch a better view of the scene. 'It looks chaotic from where I'm standing,' she confessed. 'I suppose you know what's going on!'

Ken laughed. 'I tell you, you couldn't be more mistaken. This is the best-organised job I've ever worked on in my entire life. McCabe certainly knows what he's doing. You've got to hand him that.'

But Sarah was reluctant. 'I reckon he should know what he's doing. It's his job,' she pointed out.

But it would take more than that terse, ungenerous remark to stop the Fife man in his tracks. He went on admiringly, 'And he knows how to get men to work for him, too . . .'

She somehow knew what he was going on to say.

'. . . He leads from the front, as the saying goes. He's down there now.' He nodded in the direction of the half-constructed scaffolding, though Sarah disdained to follow his eyes. 'And the men love him for it. In the experience of the people here, it's a whole new way of doing things.'

Sarah could see that would be so. The Baxters had never actually been renowned for mingling with the foot soldiers. She turned away, wishing to change the subject now. 'What was it you wanted me to see?' she smiled.

Another grin split Ken's ruddy face. 'Come inside and I'll show you,' he said.

She followed him, even more curious now. Judging by that look of pride, it wasn't just another press release. A few minutes later, as Sarah finished leafing through the papers he took from a drawer, there was a faint light of pride in her eyes, too.

'Why, this is marvellous!' she breathed.

Ken nodded. 'Just to be nominated for a design award as prestigious as this is an enormous honour in itself. If we won, it would be an inestimable feather in our caps—for Strathbiggin, for McCabe, for everyone associated with the project.'

Inestimable was the word. As Sarah ran her eye down the list of previous winners, she could appreciate the full meaning of his words. An Arabian palace, a Texan hotel. Illustrious company indeed. And if, one day, Strathbiggin's name should stand among them, it would all be down to the work of one man.

She raised her eyes tentatively to the window and stole a quick glance in the direction of the scaffolding. A mass of men in hard-hats were milling about, at first sight indistinguishable one from the other. For no good reason, she asked, 'Was he pleased to be made guest of honour at the ceilidh this year?'

Ken nodded. 'Oh, he was pleased all right.' Adding quickly, 'Will you be going?'

She shrugged. 'I don't know.'

'You will be invited, I hope?'

'Oh, yes. The editorial staff of the *Gazette* are invited every year.' It was a practice that had evolved—long before the ultra-independent McAndrew's time—when the local paper was little more than an obedient mouthpiece for the local

laird. And every year since she'd joined the *Gazette*,
Sarah had looked forward to the event. Only, this
year was different. With Brett so prominently
involved, it might be wiser to stay away. She smiled
non-committally. 'I'll see how I feel,' she said.

It was just then that the sound of a car engine
distracted her. She turned back to the window to see
a large green Volvo sweep round the side of the site
office, across the flattened, bulldozed track and come
to an abrupt, stone-skittering stop half-way to the
scaffolding.

Disapproval flitted briefly across Ken's face. 'Not
her again!' he muttered to himself. 'She's no
business going down there without permission!'

Sarah could have told him that such niceties as
requesting permission were not in this particular
visitor's repertoire. Besides, her demeanour as she
climbed out of the car, banging for attention on the
horn and waving her arms above her head, indicated
a certain presumption that permission had been
given.

What was more, the presumption appeared to be
correct. As Sarah continued to watch the scene with
almost morbid fascination, a tall, striding figure in
hard-hat and jeans detached himself from the group
of men and hurried to greet the slim, blonde girl.

Dimly, Sarah heard herself ask, 'She's been here
before, has she?'

Ken let out an impatient sigh. 'The damned
woman's never away,' he said. 'I'm expecting her to
move in here any day!'

Sarah swallowed and dropped her eyes to the file
in her hands. 'I'll borrow this, if I may,' she said

in a flat voice. 'I'm sure McAndrew will want to put a couple of paragraphs about the nomination in tomorrow's *Gazette*.'

'Sure,' Ken told her. 'Keep it as long as you like.'

She nodded. Then, unable to keep her eyes away, she glanced up at the window again—just in time to see Brett reach the car, lay one hand on Amanda's arm and bend to kiss her on the cheek. And she could see that he was smiling as Amanda slipped her arm through his.

Wretchedly, Sarah turned away, aware that her heart was thudding dully inside her chest. 'I guess I'd better be going now. Thanks for everything,' she said to Ken.

Then she walked quickly, on strange, stiff legs, out through the site-office door.

It was after eight and there was nothing to hang around for, but Sarah was in no hurry to go. She propped herself on the edge of Tom's desk and handed him a mug of tea. 'What's the story?' she asked. And she leaned to squint at the page on his typewriter as she took a mouthful from her own steaming mug.

'Just a boring old football report.' He winked good-naturedly at her, then added in a curious tone, 'Shouldn't you have gone home by now?'

She stood up. 'I had a couple of things to finish off here.' And, restlessly, she smoothed the pleats of her skirt, aware that it wasn't really true. The truth was, she was feeling unaccountably restless—and had been for the last few days. Like a loose piece of a jigsaw puzzle rattling in an empty box. She tugged her fingers through her short auburn hair and threw her colleague an appealing smile. 'How about stopping off at the Crofter's Arms for a quick drink when you've finished that?'

The grey-haired man seemed to sense her mood as he frowned back at her apologetically. 'I promised Morag I wouldn't be late. We've got visitors coming round tonight.' Then he added with a genuine smile, 'Why don't you join us? It's only the Currans—and Morag would be delighted to see you, I know.'

'Thanks, Tom.' She shook her head, knowing his invitation to be sincere, yet none the less compelled to turn it down. A quiet hour with Tom at the paper's local might have helped her to wind down a bit, but it would be inconsiderate in the extreme even to think of inflicting her current state of mind on the poor man's family and guests. 'It's time I went home myself. Uncle Dougal will be wondering where I am.'

Besides, she sensibly admonished herself as, a few minutes later, she headed for her car, it was high time she got back and had some dinner. She'd hardly eaten a thing all day. A hurried bowl of breakfast cereal, two cups of tea and half a chicken salad sandwich were literally all that had passed her lips. Hardly surprising if she felt a bit odd. Though she had to acknowledge, as she climbed behind the wheel, that she didn't feel hungry in the least. Her appetite, like her peace of mind, had suddenly deserted her.

She snapped her seat-belt into place and turned the ignition on. She was behaving ridiculously and enough was enough. This helpless, moony state of mind was out of place and out of character. She executed a swift, decisive turn and headed out of the car park to the road. She would go back to the cottage and force herself to eat a hearty three-course meal, then enjoy an hour of TV with Uncle Dougal before he went off to bed. And that, she told herself firmly, would be the end of all the silly nonsense that was cluttering up her head.

The intention was admirable, and the plan might have worked—had not fate had a surprise in store. As she came in sight of the cottage, she very nearly turned right round and drove straight back into town again. For, outside the door, as large as life, stood a wrenchingly familiar blue Range Rover.

Damn! Scowling, she drew up alongside. What the devil was he doing here? And she deliberately donned her most hostile face as she strode through the hall to the drawing-room.

He was sitting with her uncle in front of the fire, a half-empty glass of whiskey in his hand. And, foolishly, at the sight of him a tug of fierce pleasure pulled at her heart.

As he smiled, she dropped her eyes and stooped to plant a quick kiss on her uncle's cheek, suddenly irritated and perplexed by the reaction the sight of his guest had provoked. 'I'm back,' she told the old man huskily. 'Sorry I'm a bit late.'

'You work too hard.' As the craggy face creased into a welcoming smile, she felt a fleeting pang of guilt. Then she straightened defensively as he went on, 'Brett and I were just enjoying a dram. Why don't you sit down and join us, lass?'

Oh, no. She couldn't do that. Though part of her, perversely, longed to accept the invitation, all her most fearful, self-protective instincts were telling her to turn it down. Last time she and Brett had parted, they had barely been on speaking terms, so what was he doing here now? In spite of appearances, she somehow doubted it was just a social call. She shook her head, avoiding Brett's eyes. 'If you don't mind, Uncle Dougal, I won't. I really ought to have something to eat.'

'Have an aperitif first.' Before she could retreat to safety out of the door, Brett was suddenly on his feet, his tall frame filling the tiny room. He crossed to the sideboard and picked up the slim, dark bottle that was standing there, then paused to scan her face with his eyes. 'I brought round a special sherry I thought you might like. Allow me to offer you a glass.'

She hesitated, feeling trapped.

'I remembered you don't like whisky, and it's a little too early for liqueurs.' He smiled a seductive smile. 'After such a long day at the office, it'll help you to unwind.'

Such solicitude. She glanced away.

'Please, Sarah, come and join us for half an hour. I really wish you would.'

He didn't actually mean it, of course. He was simply being polite. And Sarah didn't care if he meant it or not, so why did her crazy heart skip a beat? Stiffly, she slipped off her coat and deposited it on a chair. Since he was making the effort to be civil, she might as well make the effort, too. 'OK,' she agreed uncertainly. 'Just a very small one, then.'

She watched as he deftly uncorked the bottle and helped himself to a glass from the tray, his movements easy and relaxed, with none of the self-consciousness she felt. He was dressed in a pair of navy cords, with a matching navy cashmere sweater. And the dark colour suited him, she observed—with his sun-tanned skin and jet-black hair and those long-lashed and oh, so incrediby blue eyes. Which were turned on her now as he swivelled round and held out the brimming glass to her. 'I hope it's to your taste,' he said.

As she took the glass, their fingers touched, the sensation warm, electric, achingly familiar. And as their eyes met and held for one brief, intense moment, she felt a sharp sense of regret. She had missed him, she realised suddenly.

But that was absurd. Abruptly, she lowered her eyes and took a mouthful of her drink. It was surprisingly delicious: smooth and light. Unlike any sherry she had tasted before. She composed her features and looked up at him again. 'It's very good,' she said.

He seemed pleased. 'It's a special vintage. I have a couple of cases up at the castle. If you like, you're more than welcome to one.'

She stepped back, suddenly suspicious. 'That won't be necessary,' she said. 'I'm sure one glass will be more than enough.' Then she watched through lowered lids as he turned away and sat down by the fire again. What was he up to? she asked herself.

As she perched herself on the arm of a chair, Dougal chipped in. 'Brett's been telling me about this marathon they're organising for the Easter weekend. Apparently, they're still looking for volunteers to man the stations along the route. Why don't you go along, lass, and give them a hand?'

Brett raised an eyebrow at her. 'Won't you be running?' he asked.

She shook her head. 'I wasn't planning to.' And she offered him the same excuse she'd offered her uncle. 'I've been spending too much time at my desk. I'm a little out of shape.'

He raised a dissenting eyebrow at her. 'You're fit enough, as I recall.'

She laughed at that and told him truthfully, 'If you're referring to that hike through the blizzard, my legs ached for days afterwards!' Though, normally, that wouldn't have stopped her having a go in the marathon. What was really stopping her was him. She threw him a knowing look. 'You'll be taking part, of course?'

'Of course.' He smiled. 'As sponsor, I have an example to set.'

And he would no doubt set a formidable one. She made a face. 'So, if you're down there with the runners, who's going to be handing out the prizes?' she asked.

It was the wrong question. He seemed to hesitate before answering, and she knew in a flash what he was going to say. The blue eyes narrowed slightly. 'Amanda Baxter has volunteered.'

'Of course.' He would have invited her. She felt compelled to coment, bitchily, 'Your powers of persuasion must be considerable. Surely that's slumming it a bit for her—three day eventing's more her style.'

He met her gaze steadily. 'Maybe she's branching out,' he said.

'Well, you should know.' She was trembling

absurdly as she stood up, suddenly desperately wishing that she'd followed her initial instincts and declined his offer of a drink. Why was it that in her dealings with either the Baxters or Brett the other one's name always seemed to crop up? Pointedly, she addressed herself to her uncle. 'I'll finish my drink in the kitchen, if you don't mind. It's late and I really must have something to eat.' Then, before either man could say a word, she walked swiftly across the room and disappeared out into the hall.

Safe in the sanctuary of the kitchen, she downed the sherry in one nervous gulp, then leaned against the kitchen table and took a deep breath to steady herself. Her heart was pumping, and bitter resentment was welling in her breast. Whatever his purpose, he had no right coming here—and if he had any decency, he would politely take the hint and go.

She pulled open the fridge door and helped herself to a couple of eggs. So much for her plan to treat herself to a three-course meal! A simple, straightforward omelette was about all her stomach could cope with now.

Ten minutes later, as she was sliding the omelette on to a plate, a shadow in the doorway made her turn round. It was Brett, dressed now in his leather jerkin, the collar turned up around his ears.

'I'm leaving,' he said unnecessarily. 'I've left Dougal dozing by the fire.'

So, he'd taken the hint. That was a relief. 'In that case, I'll say goodnight,' she said.

He reached in and placed the sherry bottle on the work surface near the stove. 'I thought I'd bring you this,' he said. 'Just in case you change your mind.'

She acknowledged the gesture with a stiff nod. 'Thank you,' she told him tightly. And waited for him to go.

But he didn't move. Instead, he continued to stand there with his arms folded across his chest, and there was a long, uncomfortable silence as the blue eyes and the hazel meshed. 'Before I go,' he said at last, 'I'd like a word in private with you.'

Her heart shrank. So, she'd been right, after all. This wasn't just a social call. But she kept her expression deliberately blank as, in a harsh voice, she shot back at him, 'I wasn't aware that you and I had anything to talk about—in private!'

'Wrong, Sarah.' He shook his head as a brief smile tugged at his lower lip. 'You and I could have a very great deal to talk about, if we were so inclined.'

'But we're not so inclined.' She turned away and fiddled nervously with the omelette on the plate. Why did he have to subject her to this? Why couldn't he just leave her alone and allow her to get on with her life?

But that was evidently far from being his intention now as he straightened suddenly and let his arms drop to his sides. Then, closing the door with a click behind him, he stepped decisively into the room. 'I'm sorry to disturb you. I know you're anxious to have something to eat.' There was a slight impatient edge to his voice. 'But I came here this evening specifically to see you. All I ask is a couple of minutes of your time.'

She shrugged, feigning indifference and pushed the cooling omelette aside. 'I'm not really hungry, anyway.' Even the thought of a simple omelette was too much for her stomach to cope with now. A sudden, dark anxiety had settled there like a heavy chain.

Against the pale pine of the kitchen cabinets he cast a dramatic silhouette, with his upturned collar and straight, broad shoulders and the sleek, dark hair that was spiked now with reddish lights in the reflection of the overhead lamp. He said, 'I'm sure you realised I hadn't just dropped round for a neighbourly drink.'

She eyed him aggressively. 'That's not your style.'

He smiled and continued to stand there, his expression oddly assessing as the blue eyes scanned her face. And Sarah was suddenly acutely conscious of the pulse that was ticking in her throat. She felt as though he was closing in on her. As though at any moment she might explode. She swallowed and swung round on him, eyes blazing like a cornered cat's. 'If you've got something to say, why the hell don't you just come out with it?' she spat.

He remained composed, his gaze holding hers. 'It concerns something that happened down at the site the other day.'

So, it was business. Thank God for that! 'So, why come here?' she questioned, flashing defiant anger at him. 'I deal with matters relating to work at the office, not at home!'

For a moment, he seemed to hesitate, then in a carefully measured voice he said, 'Perhaps what I want to talk about isn't entirely related to work.'

'Then, what?' She edged away, wishing he hadn't positioned himself so squarely between herself and the door, fending him off with her eyes as though he were a swarm of bees. She felt a sudden, almost physical fear that he might try to break down the barrier between them.

She saw his jaw clench, a flash of impatience spark deep in his eyes, and for a moment he seemed dangerously poised to fulfil her deepest anxieties. But the moment passed. With a brusque sigh, he dropped his eyes and moved abruptly away from the door. Then crossed the room and leaned his hips lightly against the kitchen table as he informed her quietly, 'We came very close to having an extremely serious accident at the site the other day.'

Concern jolted through her—and, at the same time, an idiotic sense of relief. He was obviously quite sound of limb, so at least no harm had come to him. 'What kind of accident?' she asked.

'The worst kind.' He bit out the words, the expression on his features suddenly harsh. 'The kind of accident that isn't really an accident at all.'

Anxiety fluttered in her throat. 'What do you mean by that?'

He sighed and ran long fingers over the surface of his hair. 'I mean that somebody, somewhere, intended for it to happen. A piece of very sensitive machinery was deliberately sabotaged. One of the mechanical elevators we use to erect the scaffolding. It functions by hydraulic power,' he explained, 'and, without going into technical details, the air-pressure control had been tampered with. Even with a minimum load—and it's habitually been loaded to maximum recently during the height of the work—the whole damned thing would have come crashing down, almost certainly killing the operator, and anyone else who was around at the time.'

Sarah's mouth had gone quite dry. It could have been him, she realised. In a hoarse voice, she demanded, 'Are you *sure* it was sabotage—not just an accident?'

He shook his head. 'It couldn't have been anything else, I'm afraid. One of the cables had been cut. If it hadn't been for the fact that I have such a damned good site manager who miraculously twigged that something was wrong, some of my men would be lying in the morgue right now and the entire project would be down the drain!

She felt herself pale. She'd never believed it could happen to him. She'd believed him inviolable, somehow. 'Good God!' she breathed. 'Who could be responsible for such a thing?'

'That, I don't know.' He smiled a grim smile. 'But one thing I can guarantee, it wasn't a well-wisher. Someone was out, not just to ground me on this project, but to shatter my entire reputation in a single blow. In all the years I've been in this business, there's never been a serious accident on any of the sites, far less a fatal one.' He let loose an oath. 'Can you imagine the carnage if Ken hadn't spotted that something was up? Apart from the tragedy of loss of life, it would have done irreparable damage to me.' He scowled angrily. 'It was definitely the work of someone with a serious grudge.'

It was a chilling thought. She frowned at him. 'Have you reported it to the police?'

'Of course. They're carrying out investigations—but they've advised me to keep quiet about the incident.' He paused and shot her a warning look. 'So, I'd be grateful if you'd treat what

I've just told you as off the record. I'd rather not have it splashed across the front page of the *Gazette*.'

She felt herself bridle at that. 'If the police have advised discretion, neither I nor my editor would consider going against that advice.' That was a policy of McAndrew's which she respected unreservedly. 'In spite of what you seem to think, I'm not totally irresponsible.'

He smiled a half-smile. 'I realise that.'

'And besides, why did you run the risk of telling me if you didn't think you could trust me?' she asked.

He regarded her through lowered lashes. 'Perhaps I knew I could,' he said.

There was a brief, tension-filled silence as he straightened and thrust his hands into the pockets of his navy cords. And some unspoken understanding seem to pass between them, far more powerful than words. Then he broke the silence and the bubble burst.

'Tell me what you know about the Imries,' he said.

It was like a bucket of cold water thrown in her face—and all at once she understood perfectly the real reason for his visit. Armed with a bottle of vintage sherry, in his usual calculating way, he'd wormed his way into this tête-à-tête quite simply to pick her brains.

She folded her arms across her chest to mask the sudden tremor in her limbs. 'I know that they're decent, hard-working folk. That's all I've ever needed to know.'

'I've heard otherwise, I'm afraid. Baxter thinks that Imrie senior was responsible for his fire.'

'And Amanda warned you against the son because you turned him down for a job, I suppose?'

He nodded curtly. 'Unfortunately, in a situation like this, one has to consider all the possibilities. The Imries would appear to have motive: revenge. But are they the type of people who would do a thing like that? That's what I'm asking.'

'I've already told you what I think.' She glared at him with hard, hostile eyes, hating him with all her strength. 'And what right do you have to come round here badgering me with questions about a family of perfectly innocent, respectable people? What right have you to make accusations without a single supporting shred of evidence?'

He was standing very still, but a warning pulse flickered deep in his eyes. 'I wasn't making accusations,' he said. 'I was simply asking a straight-forward question.'

'Liar!' She hissed the word at him. 'You and the Baxters, you're all the same! All you can think of is sticking together to protect your interests . . . ganging up on innocent people . . .! You don't care who gets hurt in the process!'

He regarded her coldly. 'Nobody's ganging up on anybody. It's all in your fevered imagination.'

'Oh, no!' She was trembling all over now, fighting to stop herself shrieking at him. 'Don't try to tell me it's all in my head. Remember, I know what a bastard and a bully you are! How you trample over anyone who gets in your way!' She wanted to destroy him. To see him crushed and torn apart—and suffering, as she was suffering.

But she knew she didn't have the power. He was

impregnable, beyond her reach. On a sudden, wild
impulse, she reached out and did what seemed like
the next best thing—grabbed hold of the sherry bottle
by the stove and smashed it viciously to the ground.

By some miracle, Dougal didn't hear the crash,
though Sarah almost wished he had. The next
instant, Brett had grabbed hold of her wrist, his
fingers an imprisoning band of steel.

'What the hell do you think you're doing?' As she
started to struggle and raised her free hand to strike
out at him, he grabbed hold of that with equal ease.
Then, with a savage twist, he anchored both her
hands in one of his, holding them impotently behind
her back. 'What the hell's got into you?'

She was pinned against him, her face mere inches
from his, and his fingers were in her hair, forcing her
to look up at him. 'You!' she hissed with angry
venom. 'Why the hell won't you leave me *alone*?'

She knew he was going to kiss her long before she
felt the crush of his lips, but she couldn't control the
jolt that went through her as his mouth made searing
contact with hers. She gasped, feeling her body go
instantly limp, the sudden rush of sensation through
her veins robbing her of the power or the will to
resist.

But it was a fierce, cruel, bruising kiss, designed to
punish, not to appease. As he released her abruptly,
she drew in breath and staggered backwards on
weak, giddy legs. 'Bastard! I hate you!' she spat.
'You deserve everything you get!' Her hand flew
protectively to her throbbing mouth. 'Get out of here!
Now! And in future, kindly keep your sexual
overtures for Amanda Baxter, who appreciates

them!'

For a long, cold moment, his eyes raked her face, so that she winced and looked away. Then, with a shrug of dismissal, he turned to the door. 'You can count on it,' he said.

CHAPTER EIGHT

SARAH had never felt less enthusiastic about a night out in her entire life. But, alas, there was no getting out of it. She'd known that from the start.

Heaven knew, she'd done her best to talk her way out of it, but her protestations had simply raised more problems than they'd solved. Dougal had eyed her narrowly. 'Are you sure you're all right, lass—in your health I mean? You haven't been yourself for the past few weeks.'

And, just the other evening, Tom had teased, 'If you miss the ceilidh on Saturday night, I'll never let you live it down. Don't you dare come and complain to me ever again that there's never any night-life in Strathbiggin!'

And so, in the interests of a quiet life—and to set her uncle's mind at rest—she had finally given up the fight and agreed, reluctantly, to go.

Now that the evening had arrived, she was regretting that decision bitterly. She glanced at the clock as she slipped her mother's lapis lazuli ear-rings into place and subjected her reflection in the mirror to a briefly appraising look. Any minute now, Tom and Morag would arrive to pick her up as arranged, and, even if she lacked the spirit, at least she was looking the part.

She was wearing her second-favourite outfit, a simple burgundy two-piece—wide, silky trousers and a belted-top—having deliberately passed over the slinky, jewel-blue dress that she had originally earmarked for the occasion. That was the dress she had worn the evening when Brett had come to dinner, and it would be associated with him now for ever in her mind. She had pushed it to the back of her wardrobe. Out of sight, out of mind. And wished a hundred bitter times that the tangled emotions in her heart could as easily be stowed away.

But they haunted her, as did the memory of that last, violent encounter with Brett. The ferocity of the emotions that had flown between them that night had left her stunned and shaken for days. The fierce, rejecting anger she had seen in his face, the destructive, inexplicable hurt that had raged like a tempest within her. Even now, almost three weeks later, it still chilled her blood to think of it.

But the eruption had finally forced her to face some truths. She'd been lying to herself. It was not hate she felt for him. And he was not the man she'd branded him.

She turned away from the dressing-table with a sigh. At least she'd been spared the torment of having to face him in the interim. As promised, she'd given the Easter marathon a wide berth and had allowed herself barely a glance at the front-page photograph of Brett—among the first five past the finishing line—receiving an enthusiastic kiss of congratulation from an even more smug-looking than usual Amanda Baxter.

And it seemed he'd been avoiding her as assiduously as she'd been avoiding him. On recent visits to the site, she'd caught not even a glimpse of him. But tonight at the ceilidh he would be there as guest of honour, in eminent prominence—and more than likely, she surmised, with Amanda Baxter on his arm. Stupidly, more than anything, it was the thought of that that caused her to dread the night ahead.

Tom was looking uncommonly spruce in full traditional Highland rig, Morag positively girlish in a flowing Laura Ashley dress; the two of them exuding the kind of enthusiasm that Sarah could only wish she felt. They stuck their heads round the cottage door to say hello to Uncle Dougal—who threw his niece a kindly wink as she pulled on her coat. 'You'll soon get in the mood once you get there,' he smiled. 'See if I'm right.'

The road to the Baxters' place wound round the outskirts of the castle estate, the site beyond the screen of trees, at this late hour, deserted and quiet. But it was there, on a dark bend of the road, that Tom's headlights picked out a lonely cyclist.

'Wasn't that young Imrie?' Morag frowned, interrupting a story about her young daughter, Susie, to swivel round curiously in her seat.

'I didn't notice.' Sarah kept her eyes fixed straight ahead, resenting the slight pull at her stomach at the mention of the Imrie name. These days, that name meant nothing but trouble, and tonight that was a commodity she could do without. She shrugged, banishing the incident from her mind. 'What were you saying about Susie?' she asked.

But, before the evening ahead was through, she would be forced to remember Morag's words.

*   *   *

The big hall of the Baxter mansion had been transformed for the occasion: the floor cleared for dancing, with a raised dais for the performers at one end, a swarm of red-clothed, candlelit tables ranged around the walls and the ceiling swathed in bands of bright tartans representing all the local clans.

Later in the evening, when the mood had mellowed and the whisky flowed, the kilted accordionist who played now would be replaced by a piper from the local pipe band. Then the room would grow still and dry eyes moist as he played his emotional repertoire of marches and laments. But for now, the mood was jolly as the couples thronged the floor for a reel, kilts swinging and the dresses of the women swirling as they swung each other round the floor.

Mr and Mrs Baxter were lined up at the door, in time-honoured fashion, to greet their guests—the latter, in spite of her finery, paling to insignificance in the shadow of the big, bluff man. Tonight, Baxter was a local hero and he was making the most of it.

With Sarah and Morag close behind, Tom cleared a path through the noisy crowd. 'I'll get us a drink,' he announced as he tracked down an empty table and invited the two women to sit down. But as the music slowed to a stately strathspey, Morag grasped him excitedly by the arm.

'Let's dance this one first,' she urged. Then turned to Sarah with an appealing smile. 'You don't mind, do you?'

'Of course not.' Sarah smiled back and shook her head. How could she possibly stand in the way of such obvious connubial bliss?

She followed them wistfully with her eyes as they made their way between the tables to the floor. It was somehow both a pleasure and a pain to see two people so happy together. And it was then, as the crowd parted to let them pass, that she caught her first heart-stopping glimpse of the tall, striking couple in the centre of the floor.

Amanda was wearing a vivid green dress. Floor-length, backless, stunningly cut. Her long hair had been drawn back into a stylish, shining blonde chignon, and there was a look of radiance on her face.

It was not difficult to see why. Her smiling, attentive partner was, without a shadow of a doubt, the most handsome man in the entire room, a dark and elegant figure in an immaculately tailored dinner-suit, black hair swept back from his high, bronzed forehead, a smile of total self-assurance curving the finely moulded lips. At the sight of him, Sarah's heart gave a sickening jolt, yet she could not tear her eyes away. She watched with a helpless sense of loss as the crowd closed round once more and Brett was abruptly swallowed from view.

The evening proceeded on its disastrous way, more or less as she'd known it would. As far as possible, she kept off the dance-floor and stayed at the table, out of sight. She was in no mood for dancing—especially with Brett and Amanda out there together at every turn. Though he'd managed to tear himself away, she'd noticed, for an old-fashioned waltz with Amanda's mother. Quite clearly, these days, he was virtually part of the family.

But at least there was one thing to be grateful for. He'd been so preoccupied with Amanda all evening, he probably hadn't even noticed that Sarah was there.

Tom and Morag were having the time of their lives. Sarah watched with an envious smile a they trooped on to the dance-floor yet again, then lowered her eyes abruptly as she caught sight of Ken moving in her direction, just as the tempo slowed. She had noticed him earlier and had known that it was just a matter of time before he came over to claim a dance. But, as much as she liked him, she would rather stay put. Perhaps if she pretended not to see him and stared down at the floor . . .

The ruse didn't work. A shadow had fallen over her chair. Forcing a polite smile, she glanced up—and felt her heart trip headlong in her chest as she found herself looking into Brett's bronzed face.

'May I have the pleasure?' He smiled and extended a hand to her.

Shakily, she got to her feet, wishing she didn't feel quite so ridiculously pleased, then sort of floated on to the floor, feeling his touch like fire on the back of her arm. He guided her round to face him and she felt her heart stop in her breast as one hand stole round to circle her waist and he drew her softly against his chest.

This is just a duty dance, she kept telling herself, but somehow it still felt like a dream.

They danced without speaking at first, their silence, like a private capsule, drawing them closer, above the crowd. She could hear her heart thudding, feel his breath against her cheek, as their bodies moulded, moving across the floor, effortlessly as one.

He told her in a soft voice, 'I think you've been hiding from me.'

Her mouth was dry. 'Hiding? Have I?'

'You shouldn't.' His grip seemed to tighten a little. 'You know it's a waste of time.'

Dumbly, Sarah shook her head, suddenly knowing nothing at all.

'I can always track you down.'

'Why should you want to?' she asked.

She felt him smile and his jaw brushed lightly against her hair. 'Because you're my very own private reporter—or had you forgotten that?'

He was teasing. Perhaps even gently poking fun. But she didn't care. She just wanted to stay there in his arms, drowning in his warmth, in the scent of him. She stole a glance at the straight, dark profile. 'I thought you'd be wearing the kilt tonight.'

He laughed—and it suddenly seemed to Sarah's ears like an eternity since she'd heard that sound. 'I was tempted,' he confessed. 'But in the end I decided to opt for a more conventional form of dress.'

'You mean you got cold feet,' she teased.

He gave her midriff a playful squeeze. 'Are you disappointed?' he asked.

She couldn't be that. Just the sight of him was joy enough. But that was her secret. She looked into his eyes. 'Maybe,' she said.

He smiled again and drew her close. 'OK,' he told her. 'Some other time.'

It was a totally meaningless remark, not meant to signify a thing. But, though she knew that, she felt her heart give a little bound. If only, she found herself thinking—and closed her eyes, daring to smile with quiet happiness as his body pressed against her and one hand moved gently upwards to caress the sensitive skin of her neck. If only the music would never stop and this magic moment never end.

But it did, too soon. As they came to a stop in the middle of the room, his hand seemed to linger on her waist—almost, she thought, in sudden, reckless hope, as though he might invite her to dance some more.

But it was just at that very moment that the pale-faced man came bursting into the room.

Gesticulating almost dementedly, he forced his way through the crowd to the dais. 'Mr McCabe!' he yelled, his eyes like beacons as he searched the room. 'Come quickly, for God's sake—there's a fire at the site! The whole bloody place has gone up in flames!'

What followed was an uproar. Suddenly, everyone was shouting at once as the man's words were repeated around the room. Sarah saw Brett's face go suddenly pale beneath the darkness of his tan. 'I knew it!' he muttered beneath his breath. Then, even as she reached out to touch his arm, he was elbowing his way through the crowd to the door.

For a moment, she was too shocked to move. Then her journalist reflexes came to her rescue and she, too, was racing across the room, heading for the nearest phone. She got straight through to McAndrew. 'Get a photographer down to McCabe's place right away,' she told him. 'It seems the arsonist has struck again.'

Then she was barging her way back through the crowd, searching for Tom. He was at her elbow at once. 'I'll give you a lift,' he said.

The man hadn't been exaggerating. The site was a fireball, belching thick, black fumes, with sheets of flames as high as mountains visible for miles. Everything that could be had been set alight—all the new buildings, equipment and materials consumed in a raging inferno that lit up the entire sky.

'My God!' Tom breathed, and Sarah felt a sudden, angry nausea as she climbed out of the car. The arsonists had been foiled in their attempt to destroy the Baxters' place, but this time they'd done a cruelly efficient job.

It was then that Sarah remembered the lonely cyclist they'd passed on the way to the ceilidh that night. 'Wasn't that young Imrie?' Morag had asked. And Sarah shivered now at the thought. It looked as though Baxter had been absolutely right about the Imries all along.

The job that had to be done that night was the most unpalatable of her career—taking statements from fire officers, lookers-on and police—with one eye all the time on the figure of Brett. Still in his dinner-jacket, he stood to one side, alone, surveying the catastrophe with a stricken expression on his face. And, in spite of all the many differences that had divided them in the past, Sarah felt her heart unreservedly go out to him. Whatever else he might deserve, he didn't deserve a blow like this.

It was past midnight by the time the fire brigade finally managed to douse the flames. In the searchlights, all that remained of what had once been a vibrant, throbbing place was a pile of twisted girders and a few heaps of blackened rubble strewn across the wasteland like the ugly stumps of rotten teeth.

Sickened, Sarah turned away. Those responsible

for this terrible thing were conscience and evil men. There was no grudge or sense of injury that could justify a foul deed such as this.

'Shall I give you a lift home?' All at once, Tom was at her side, an understanding hand on her arm.

She shook her head wearily. 'No, off you go. I still have to phone in my report.' She smiled a weak smile. 'Besides, you've already stayed long enough. Morag will be wondering where you are.'

The grey-haired man smiled back at her. 'Don't worry, Morag won't be complaining,' he said. 'She's been married to a journalist too long for that.' Then he added kindly, 'I don't mind waiting for you, you know.'

'I know—but you don't have to.' Sarah had been grateful for him sticking around. Amidst all the horror, his calm, canny presence had been comforting. But she could easily manage to get home by herself. 'There are plenty of people to give me a lift,' she assured him, nodding to the groups of people still gathered round in small, concerned knots. 'You go on back to your wife.'

'You're sure?'

'I'm sure.'

'OK.' He nodded and started to turn away, then paused with a sigh to shake his head. 'This is a sad, sad day for Strathbiggin,' he said.

Once, Sarah would not have agreed with him—but that time felt now like a lifetime ago. As she trudged through the rubble to the castle, she was filled with a sense of outrage and disgust. Out there somewhere were some sick and evil men who must be made to pay for what they had done. Until they were brought to justice, their deeds cast a dark and guilty shadow over the whole community.

The back door was open and most of the lights appeared to be on. She slipped into the hall, closing the door behind her, and glanced round. 'Brett!' she called quietly. But there was no answer. Maybe he was still outside. Maybe he didn't wish to be disturbed.

She went through to the office to make her call—there seemed no need to request permission in the circumstances—quickly assembled her scribbled notes and read out her report to the waiting sub. McAndrew cut in just as she was about to hang up the phone. 'Well done, Sarah,' he told her in a rare burst of praise. 'Go home now and have the sleep you deserve.'

But Sarah hadn't finished yet. Without quite knowing what she wanted to say to him, she knew she couldn't leave without seeing Brett. And, though he hadn't responded when she'd called, she was almost certain he was here in the house.

She stuffed her hands nervously into the pockets of her coat and stepped tentatively out into the hall. He wasn't in his bedroom; there was no light coming from under the door. Unless, of course, he was asleep—an unlikely event in the circumstances. But there were lights on in the room at the end of the hall, and something told her she would find him there. She crept forward, feeling her heart thump in her chest, and cautiously poked her head round the door.

It was a big room. Elegantly furnished, with a carved oak fireplace at one end where a log fire was burning in the grate. A high-backed armchair had been drawn up in front of the fire and a tall, lean figure in a dark dinner-suit was seated there, long legs stretched out in front of him, totally still. And, though his face and head were hidden by the obscuring wings of the dark leather chair, she could guess at the brooding expression he wore as he stared unblinking into the flames.

At the sight of him, her heart turned over. He looked so alone, so desolate. Yet, though she longed to go to him, she hung back in the doorway, feeling like an intruder on his private grief.

But he had heard her, though he didn't turn round. 'What do you want?' His voice was harsh.

She stepped forward apologetically. 'I've come to say I'm sorry,' she said.

'Sorry? For what?' He half turned round to look at her, his features an impenetrable mask of steel.

'I'm sorry about what happened tonight. About the fire, of course.'

'Of course!' He turned away with a bitter, scoffing laugh and waved a dismissive hand at her. 'Save it, Sarah,' he bit out. 'The party's over. Go home to bed.'

She hesitated, regarding the implacable profile with a mixture of trepidation and concern. Then, in a deliberate gesture, she slipped off her coat, laid it on a chair and walked over to him. 'Brett, are you all right?' she asked.

'All right?' He threw her a sarcastic look. 'I wouldn't say it's the best I've ever been. More than two years of planning and hard work have just literally gone up in flames.' He laughed hollowly at the irony. 'But I'm not about to tear out my hair or throw myself into the loch. So, if you've come to gloat, you can go home now. This is all you're going to get.'

She stepped forward across the soft grey carpet, her heart tight with emotion inside her chest. 'I haven't come here to gloat. I'm sorry, genuinely sorry. Please believe that,' she said. And there was an almost pleading note in her voice as he raised one sceptical eyebrow at her. 'If you're thinking about what I said that night, I didn't mean it and I'm sorry about that, too.'

She had secretly longed to tell him that, to unburden herself of the guilt she felt. And finally to acknowledge out loud what it had taken her too long to realise. 'I've been wrong about you from the start, and I apologise.'

He looked away and, in a weary gesture, drew one hand across his brow. 'Well, none of that matters much any more. In a very short time, you'll be shot of me.'

'What do you mean?'

He leaned his head against the back of the chair and narrowed his eyes at her. 'It means that I'm packing up, pulling out—whatever you want to call it,' he said.

'You mean you're going back to Canada?'

'You've got it in one. Just as soon as I can wind things up here, I'll be on the first plane home.'

She stared at him, astounded. 'And what about the project?' she wanted to know.

'The project?' He shrugged. 'Forget it. It's jinxed. First the elevator, then this fire. I can't run risks like that with my employees' lives. No, what I intend to do is fold up this whole disastrous project, put the castle and estate on the market and just forget about the whole damned thing.' As a frown of protest crossed her face, he responded with a cynical look. 'Don't worry, the workers who have lost their jobs will all be generously compensated.'

But, for once, that wasn't what she was thinking of. She straightened her shoulders. 'You can't do that.'

'Oh, but I can,' he assured her. 'And I will.'

'You can't. She walked right up to the edge of his chair and looked down at him indignantly. 'I'm sorry, but you have no right.'

'No right?' He regarded her with wry amusement. 'And what is that supposed to mean?'

'It means that you have no right to come here with all your plans and promises of a new life for the people here. To put the dream within their grasp, and then just to snatch it away.' Her limbs were suddenly trembling, but her voice was firm. 'The people of Strathbiggin are relying on you to help them make something better of their lives, to build a future for themselves and their children, and you don't have the right to take it away from them now.'

She swallowed and continued, ignoring the look of surprise on his face, 'I was wrong about a lot of things at the start and I don't mind admitting it now. Strathbiggin was a dead place before you came. Now it's come back to life again. There's hope and vitality today where there was only despair before. It would be a wicked and terrible thing if you were to take that away.' She paused, only now, as she came to the end of her emotional discourse, realising that she'd meant every word of it. 'We need you, Brett. Strathbiggin needs you. Surely that means something to you.'

For a long, poignant moment, her words hung suspended in the air, and the only sound was the crackle of the fire as they gazed, without speaking, into one another's eyes. Then Brett said, 'Unfortunately, it would appear that not everyone agrees with you.'

'Because of the fire? That was the work of some crazy, spiteful individual. That wasn't the people of Strathbiggin talking.' She recounted the story of the cyclist and how she'd already reported the incident to the police. 'Whoever it was must be caught and punished—but, whatever you do, don't give them the satisfaction of letting them see that they've beaten you. That's what they want. Don't give in to them.'

He smiled ruefully and shook his head. 'That's easy for you to say. You haven't just seen a personal dream reduced to ashes in front of your eyes.'

But she would not give in. 'It can still happen, Brett. It'll just take a little more time.' She kept her eyes fixed on his face. 'Think of that design award you've been nominated for. Have you any idea just how much that means to the people here?'

'Believe it or not, it means a great deal to me as well.' His eyes held hers. 'I was serious right now when I said this project was a personal dream. I've put my heart and soul into it. It means more to me than anything I've ever done before.'

She could see from his eyes that it was true. 'Then do it,' she said.

There was a pause, then, quite unexpectedly, he leaned forward in his seat and held out both hands to her. A smile touched his lips. 'Come here,' he said.

Almost shyly, she obeyed, feeling her breath stop

in her throat as his fingers closed over hers. She dropped to her knees in front of him as he drew her down. 'Promise me you'll go ahead with the scheme.'

He smiled again and reached out to touch her hair. 'OK, I promise. Just for you.'

'You mean it?'

'I mean it.' He was drawing her close. 'But tomorrow,' he told her gruffly, 'not tonight.'

For one desperate, endless moment, she felt as though she couldn't breathe, then the whole world suddenly seemed to tilt as his lips came down to cover hers.

There was no resistance in her now, no more conflict in her heart. All of that had fled from her like the memory of a bad dream. She closed her eyes and wound her arms lovingly around his neck, letting her fingers trail with delight through the thick, dark hair at the nape of his neck. And she sighed and let her body press meltingly against his, her senses shivering in aching response as he caressed her with his fingertips.

The silky top slid easily from the waistband of her trousers, and his touch was like fire against her skin as he deftly undid the hook of her bra. Then his grip tightened possessively as he leaned back to look into her face. 'Sarah, don't go home tonight. Stay here with me.'

Her breath froze. For ever, she thought, and let out a helpless sigh as he drew her into his arms again and his hand swept round to caress her breast. It was a wild, impossible, crazy thought, she knew that before it had even formed in her head. Tonight was the only time together that she and Brett would ever have. That was the way it was written. That was the way it had to be. But tonight, at least, he could be hers, and that opportunity was too precious to waste. She moaned and pressed her lips to his face, filled with a lifetime of wanting him.

He drew her down on to the thick, soft rug, simultaneously shedding his jacket and tie, then unbuttoned the buttons of his white dress-shirt and gently guided her hand inside. The flat, hard planes of his hair-roughened chest felt delicious against the palm of her hand, and as she grazed her fingers against the blunt male nipples, she heard him expel a shuddering sigh.

In the flicker of the fire, he peeled each garment—and, with them, her inhibitions—away, tutoring her unschooled but willing hands in the art of performing the same for him. At last, they lay naked, burning in the fire of each other's desire. In the soft light, the deep bronze of his skin contrasted with the ivory of hers, the spare, hard, masculine lines of him with the rounded, feminine curves of her.

'Trust me.'

'I do.'

He leaned and kissed her, a deep, urgent kiss, seeming to brand her lips with his, his fingers teasing her upturned nipples, whipping her senses to a storm. Then smoothing, caressing the round of her hips, the curve of her belly, the bloom of her thighs. Causing the breath to catch in her throat as the rhythm of his stroking fingers increased and she felt his hand gently part her thighs.

She had never been touched like this before, never been loved as he was loving her now. And he seemed to know instinctively every intimate move her body craved, every subtle stroke, every pause, every pressure. His hands were the hands of a sorcerer.

Then, at last, as the spiral inside her tightened almost unbearably and her head lashed helplessly from side to side, she felt the swift race of his heart against hers as he pulled himself on top of her. Both hands were on her breasts as he bent to take crushing possession of her lips, then she gasped and let out a shuddering moan as she felt him become a part of her.

There was no pain, just a warm and gratifying sensation that, suddenly, she was complete. She clung to him, letting her body move with his, slowly at first, then with increasing urgency, as the coil of desire inside her tightened, longing for release. Then she cried out, her hands in his hair, as with one, final, penetrating thrust he swept them both into the shimmering void.

Much later, he carried her through to his room down the hall, to the big, gold-silk-covered bed. With a feeling of peace and contentment that she had never known before, she nestled against him between the soft, cool sheets, and finally fell into a dreamless sleep in the safe, warm circle of his arms.

Next morning, she awoke with a smile on her lips and, with a sigh of contentment, stretched out her arm. But there was no one there. The sheets were cold.

She sat up abruptly and looked round the big,

strange room with its gold-pile carpet and fridge and
cocktail cabinet ranged alongside the bed, suddenly
feeling uncomfortably like an alien. Where was Brett?
How long had he been gone? And why hadn't he
wakened her?

On a chair at the foot of the bed, she could see that
her clothes had been neatly piled, and a soft, self-
conscious flush touched her cheeks as she
remembered how eagerly they had been shed last
night. And how they had been left in casual
abandonment, strewn across the drawing-room floor.
Brett must have discreetly gathered them up and
brought them in here while she was asleep.

She showered quickly and dressed, suddenly
feeling incongruous in the silky trousers and top of
last night. Then she pulled open the curtains and
peered outside, observing that Brett's Range Rover
had gone as well. She frowned at her watch. It was
half-past eight on a Sunday morning. Surely he
couldn't have gone far?

Outside, the first person she saw was Ken. Hiding
her embarrassment, she hurried up to him. 'Good
morning,' she smiled, and shoved her hands into the
pockets of her coat and tried to sound casual as she
enquired, 'Have you see Brett? Is he around?'

If he was surprised to see her, he was much too
discreet to give any sign—or to make any comment
on the implications of her attire. But she thought she
sensed a momentary hesitancy as he replied, 'I saw
him earlier, but he left about half an hour ago.'

'Where to?'

Ken shook his head. 'He didn't say.' And turned
away as though to go.

'Did he say when he'd be back?'

It was then that she began to realise how foolishly impetuous she'd been. If she'd been wise, she would have taken the opportunity of Brett's absence to slink off home and put last night behind her, like the fleeting dream that it had been. But she'd clung on like a desperate fool and allowed her reckless heart to hope.

Ken's answer to her question was far more crushing, far more cruel than he'd ever intended it to be. 'I think he'll be gone for quite some time. He went off with Amanda Baxter, you see.'

CHAPTER NINE

DECLINING Ken's offer of a lift, she walked home, suddenly preferring to be alone. And was relieved, when she got back to the cottage, to see that there was no one at home. Dougal had probably gone out with the dog.

Moving like an automaton, she hung up her coat, shed the silky burgundy two-piece and pulled on her towelling robe. Then frowned at her reflection in the mirror and dragged her fingers through her hair. Hadn't she known it would end like this? So, why this crushing sense of despair? Of course he'd gone off with Amanda. Hadn't she always known the score?

She turned away, gulping back tears. At least she didn't regret last night. The memory of how he had loved her was one she would carry with joy to her grave. What she did regret, and bitterly now, was everything that had gone before. She would reproach herself till the end of her days for all the disastrous mistakes she'd made.

She stabbed her feet into pink velvet slippers and fought back the pain that tore at her heart. If only she'd taken more time to know him. If only she hadn't been so quick to condemn. She'd been wrong about everything right from the start, and she only had herself to blame. And the knife inside her twisted as she acknowledged the cruellest blunder of all. He

was the only man she would ever love, and yet she
had deliberately driven him into another woman's
arms.

She forced a shrug as tears pricked her eyes. She
would just have to learn to live with it. And at least
she would have the satisfaction of knowing he'd
promised to go ahead with his scheme. In spite of her
own deep personal sorrow, she would know that
some good had come out of all this.

She went through to the bathroom and emptied
bubble bath into the bath, then turned on the taps,
slipped off her robe and hung it on the back of the
door. A long, hot, soothing soak, that was what she
needed now. She sank into the bubbles, closed her
eyes and wished she were a million miles away.

But there was no escape from the troubled thoughts
that came crowding into her brain. The thought that
he was with Amanda, the fear that she might never
see him again. And the madness of the argument
she'd used all along to push him away. For she knew
now that there was no divide. Last night had finally
opened her eyes. She had never before, and would
never again, feel such closeness with another human
being.

She shivered. Perhaps, deep down in her soul, she
had always known the truth—but fear had caused her
to deny it, knowing the terrible risk to her heart
should she end up loving, then losing him.

And she had lost, and she must pay the cost—and
she knew what part of the cost must be. She must
leave Strathbiggin as soon as she could and never,
never come back again.

Resolutely, she swallowed. It would be a wrench,

but she had no choice. With Brett all around to haunt her, there could be no life for her here any more. Somehow, from somewhere, she must find the strength to rebuild her shattered life elsewhere.

At that moment, the front door opened and there was the sound of footsteps in the hall. 'I'm in the bath, Uncle Dougal!' she called out, hastily composing herself. 'I'll be through in a little while!' She sighed and leaned back and closed her eyes. After all these years, she would miss the old man.

That sad thought was as far as she got. A moment later, her heart lurched to her throat as a hand grappled roughly with the door-handle. Then she stiffened in horror as the door was flung wide and Brett came striding into the room. He stood over her, scowling. 'What the hell do you think you're doing?' he ground out in a deep, harsh voice.

She coloured and sank up to her chin in the bubbles. 'I'm the one who should be asking that!'

But he was in no mood for bandying words. 'Why the devil couldn't you just wait for me back at the house?' he rasped. He grabbed a towel from the towel rail and flung it unceremoniously at her. 'Get out of there and come through to the kitchen. At once! I want to talk to you!'

As Sarah clutched the towel to her bosom and prudishly remained where she was, the glimmer of a comprehending smile momentarily lightened the scowl on his face. Last night, he had explored with his hands and his eyes every trembling inch of her, but he was enough of a gentleman, for the moment, to respect her sudden need for privacy.

'I'll give you exactly one minute!' he warned, and

strode quickly back out through the door.

Rarely had she moved so fast. She was dried and back in her towelling robe in forty-seven seconds flat. Bewildered and anxious at this unexpected twist, she stuck her head round the kitchen door.

He was standing by the table with his arms folded impatiently across his chest. She felt the knot in her stomach clench. 'Well, what do you want?' she asked.

He didn't move, but with a nod of his head indicated one of the chairs. 'I want you to sit down,' he said.

'Why?' For a moment she paused, then, correctly interpreting the look in his eye, decided to do as she was told. 'Perhaps you wouldn't mind explaining what the meaning of all this is?'

He hooked his hands into the pockets of his jeans and leaned against the cabinet, eyeing her. 'It might interest you to know,' he informed her slowly, 'that I've just come from the Baxters' place.'

She'd guessed that, and it wasn't a thought that enraptured her soul. 'Where you've been is your business,' she shot back defensively at him.

An indecipherable expression crossed his eyes. 'Nevertheless, I'm sure you'd be interested to hear the reason why I was there.'

She herself was not so sure. She swallowed on the painful lump in her throat. 'Something, I've no doubt, to do with the daughter of the house.'

'Not the daughter.' He shook his head. 'More the father, as a matter of fact.' He straightened and frowned down at her. 'In the early hours of this morning, old man Baxter was arrested,' he said.

'Arrested? Baxter?' Like an idiot, she repeated the words. It was the last piece of news she'd expected to hear. She blinked at him, scarcely able to believe her ears. 'On what charge?' she wanted to know.

'A double charge of arson. And deliberate, malicious sabotage.'

She blinked again. 'You mean——?'

He nodded, his expression grim. 'Yes, Baxter was responsible for the fire at the site last night—and it was his men who tampered with the elevator. He was also, needless to say, responsible for the fire at his own house.'

It was almost more than Sarah could take in. 'But what about the Imries?' she frowned. 'I thought they were the guilty ones?'

'That was what Baxter wanted us to think. He deliberately set the Imries up. You see, what he really wanted was to get rid of me—and that public squabble he had with Imrie, when Imrie was imprudent enough to make a threat, offered him an irresistible opportunity. A fire at his place could be blamed on Imrie, then suspicion whipped up that I might be next. The Imries have a reputation for being a bit troublesome. As fall guys, they were pretty well made to measure.'

Brett paused and ran a hand across his hair. 'But what Baxter didn't reckon on was that they wouldn't go down without a fight. They'd heard rumours about what he was up to and they decided to keep an eye on the site. When Morag saw young Imrie on his bike last night, that's exactly what he was doing, in fact.' He uttered an oath. 'Unfortunately, they weren't able to spot Baxters' men in time, but they

did see them make their getaway—and later
identified each and every one of them to the police.'
He smiled a brief, contemptuous smile. 'Needless to
say, honour among thieves being what it is, the very
first thing that they all did was point the finger at
their boss.'

Sarah's brain was in a whirr. It all seemed so
patently obvious now, and yet she'd never suspected
a thing. 'But why?' She frowned across at him in
concern. 'Why would Baxter do such a thing?'

He shrugged. 'He had two reasons, I suppose. One
was to collect the insurance money—which he was
badly in need of to pay off his debts. The Baxters, I'm
afraid, have got used to a life-style that they ceased to
be able to afford a long time ago. But the money
wasn't his principal motivation. His main aim, as I
said, was to try to persuade me to leave. His sagging
finances were bad enough, but what he couldn't
handle at all was that fact that, with my arrival on the
scene, he was no longer kingpin around these parts.
He hated me for it. Sure, he put on a convincing
show. But, personally, I was never in any doubt
about what his true feelings were.'

'You mean you suspected him all along?'

'I always knew he was a potential threat.' He threw
her a mysterious look. 'You don't go into a venture
like this without first finding out who your enemies
are. Believe me——' his lips curled with obvious
distaste '—I didn't accept Baxter's overtures out of
any liking for the man—but there's a saying my old
Scottish grandmother taught me: keep your friends
close, but your enemies closer. I believe there's a lot
of wisdom in that.'

Sarah smiled to herself, remembering with irony how Dougal had once quoted that very same maxim in reference to him. Then her expression sobered. 'What about Amanda? How does she fit into all of this?'

He sighed, shifted position and folded his arms across his chest. 'It seems that the lovely Amanda was playing a double game. She knew what her father was up to—they're as thick as thieves—but that didn't stop her one little bit from trying to make up to me. I guess she wanted it both ways—the family position restored and, as an added bonus, a financially lucrative match for herself.'

He drew in breath. 'That was why she came rushing round to the castle first thing this morning—to salvage at least one part of her plan by somehow persuading me that she'd never actually known anything at all about what was going on. An unscrupulous young lady I'd say. I was subjected to quite a performance back there at the family home. I didn't believe a word anyway, but, unfortunately for Amanda, her mother walked in on her little act and promptly blew the gaff on her. When I left half an hour ago, the two of them were at each other's throats.'

So, the worm had turned! At least, there was some satisfaction in knowing that.

He was still standing, regarding her through lowered lids, a curiously watchful expression on his face. And Sarah's head was suddenly clamouring with questions that must be asked. She took a deep breath and cleared her throat. 'Were you very disappointed—about Amanda—when you found out?'

He didn't move. 'It's always disappointing to discover that someone had been lying to you.'

Her heart was hammering. 'Especially when you happen to care for that someone,' she pointed out.

He raised an enquiring eyebrow at her. 'Why do you say that?' he asked.

It was a tremendous effort to keep her voice steady, but somehow—just—Sarah managed it. 'All those evenings you spent together. All those cosy little dinners.'

'A couple of dinners at her parents' place. I was inveigled into them.'

'What about that evening at the Neuk Inn? Surely you weren't inveigled into that?'

He smiled. 'Your sources were wrong about that, you know. I went there alone, as a matter of fact. Amanda came in with a group of friends and insisted on detaching herself from them and joining me. I didn't invite her. She invited herself. There wasn't really a great deal I could do.'

Sarah had scarcely moved a muscle since he'd first started to speak, and her gaze had not for one single second flickered from his face. But she felt her shoulders give an involutary jerk and, nervously, she looked away as he came across to the table now and pulled up a chair on the other side. 'You know,' he was saying, 'we could have cleared all this up long ago. That evening a few weeks ago, when I came round to the cottage, I told you I wanted to speak to you—but somehow I never got round to saying what I'd really come to say.'

He paused and she could feel his eyes on her face, though, still, she did not look up. And her heart was in turmoil inside her chest as he went on to explain, 'I knew you'd seen Amanda at the site that afternoon, and I guessed at the impression you'd probably got. I wanted to tell you then that there was nothing going on between Amanda and me. Never had been, never could be. In spite of everything you've always said, I'm afraid she's really not my type.

'But, as I said, unfortunately, I never got that far. Somehow, in our usual fashion, we ended up in a fight.' He drew his breath in sharply between his teeth. 'And that was when I more or less decided there was no hope for us. God knows, you'd made it plain enough that you weren't interested. I decided it would be better for both of us if I just kept well away from you.'

A cry of protest jammed in her throat. She shook her head dumbly, unable to speak.

'Until last night.' He reached across the table and took one of her hands in his, then tilted her chin with his fingertips and forced her to look into his eyes. 'Last night, I definitely got the impression that maybe I was wrong, after all.'

She blushed and would have looked away again, but, with a firm hand, he held her there. 'Sarah, a long time ago, I told you something about myself. About how I'd come here looking for two things—my roots and, possibly, a wife. I suppose you thought that was a corny idea. I thought it was pretty corny myself. I guess that, really, deep down, I'm still just a romantic Scot at heart. But, corny or not, the fact is that I found the girl I was looking for within twenty-four hours of arriving here. She was the redhead I spotted on my video climbing in through the site-office window.'

Her heart stopped. Then her eyes widened as she gaped at him in disbelief. 'How on earth can you say that? You were after my blood!' she cried.

He shook his head at her and smiled. 'Once I'd checked you out and confirmed you weren't working for Baxter, I knew you weren't any threat to me.'

'But you virtually blackmailed me!' she protested. 'What about the tape?'

'I destroyed the tape immediately after our first interview. You could have written anything about me you liked; I wouldn't have had anything to come back at you with.'

'You tricked me!'

He smiled a hard smile, reminiscent of earlier days. 'I wasn't about to let you off the hook so easily. You deserved a bit of a fright.' Then his features softened as he reached out and caught hold of her other hand. 'But don't try and lead me off the subject again. You may not be aware of it, young woman, but this man has just proposed to you.'

She blinked at him.

'I love you, Sarah. Very much. Please say you'll marry me.'

She didn't have a chance to say a thing. There was a sudden crash out in the hall, then the kitchen door swung open and Uncle Dougal came bursting in. He glanced from one to the other with a look of triumph on his face. 'Have you heard the news?' he beamed. 'Old man Baxter's in the nick!'

Shakily, Sarah got to her feet, beaming with a happiness of her own. 'I have a much more important

announcement to make,' she told him, almost
bursting with pride. And she reached for the hand of
the man at her side and smiled with love into his
eyes. 'There's going to be a wedding, Uncle Dougal,'
she said. 'I'm happy for you to be the first to
know—I've just agreed to marry Brett.'

It was the biggest, grandest wedding that
Strathbiggin had ever seen, and Sarah was the
happiest, most radiant bride. Half the town had
turned out to throw rice and confetti outside the
church, and the local pipe band played an
impromptu salute as the couple drove off on their
honeymoon. As Dougal had remarked with a tear in
his eye, no two people could ever have embarked on
a life together with more good wishes to speed them
on their way.

The year that had slipped by since then had been
for Sarah a kind of rebirth. There had been so much
to discover, so much to learn—about herself and the
man she loved. And with Brett beside her every step
of the way, she had finally found her place in the
world.

Though it was not the world she had known
before. It was a bigger, far more exciting place. For
the horizons of two people together, she had
discovered, were infinitely broader than the horizons
of one.

The broadening of horizons had been both
geographical and personal. These days, Brett's home
in Toronto and his ranch up in the Lakes felt almost
as much like home to Sarah as Strathbiggin had ever
been. And she had grown to love them as she loved

the man who had brought them into her life—with a fierce, proud, passionate love that grew more unshakeable every day. At times, it was hard to imagine that he had not always been a part of her life.

It had been good to come back to Strathbiggin for their first anniversary. To see Dougal, who was thriving quite happily in the care of Mrs Campbell, and to share with Tom and McAndrew the professional satisfaction of her new role as editor of her very own brainchild, The McCabe company magazine—'a totally autonomous position', as Brett had insisted when she'd taken it on. 'I don't even want to know what's going in it until I see it in print!'

She glanced across at him now as they drew up at a strategic position at the head of the glen with a panoramic view out over Loch Coih, her heart filled with deep contentment as he reached across and took her hand.

'Well, what do you think?'

She reached up and kissed his cheek. 'I think I can scarcely believe my eyes.'

'Well, you'd better.' He kissed her back. 'I promise you, this is for real.' He nodded to the miracle that was spread out below. 'With the conversion of the castle now complete and most of the additional buildings in place, we can expect our first influx of visitors later this month. I'm even told that, for the summer, we're already almost fully booked.'

She hugged his arm, sharing the pride she could hear in his voice. 'All that publicity we got for winning the design award obviously didn't do any harm.'

'None at all.' He winked at her. 'Now the public

can come and discover for themselves why we're the best damned leisure centre in the British Isles.'

Sarah sighed happily. So much had changed. And all for the better, it seemed. Here in Strathbiggin, with Baxter in prison and Amanda flown, the rule of the Baxters had come to an end. She leaned her head against Brett's shoulder. 'You know, I was just thinking how lucky I am. I have two more homes than I had this time last year—and one more person to love.' As her eyes flicked round to the carry-cot in the back seat of the car that held their precious two-month-old son, she felt a sudden quickening in her heart. Even dreams she'd never even dared to dream, with Brett around were coming true.

He kissed her hair and joked, 'If that's not enough, we can easily arrange for more.'

'Homes or babies?'

'Whichever you prefer.'

'I think I have enough homes for now.'

'Be careful,' he grinned. 'I might just decide to take you up on that.'

'Any time.' She smiled at him and leaned to plant a warm kiss on his lips. 'I love you very much,' she said.

'I love you, too.'

It was the millionth time she'd heard him say those words, but still they sent a wrench of delight through her. She clung to him as his arms went round her, and for a long, breathless moment, the world stood still.

Then, slowly, the big car nosed out on to the road and, together, the three of them drove back home.

The Christmas present you won't want to part with.

Four great new titles in a seasonal gift pack for only £5.00. Long dark evenings of reading by a blazing fire. Will you keep it or will you give it away?

TRUE PARADISE_____Catherine George
TAKEOVER MAN_____Vanessa Grant
TUSCAN ENCOUNTER_____Madeleine Ker
DRIVING FORCE_____Sally Wentworth

Published October 1988   Price £5.00

YOU'RE INVITED TO ACCEPT **FOUR ROMANCES** AND A TOTE BAG **FREE!**

Acceptance card

NO STAMP NEEDED | Post to: Reader Service, FREEPOST, P.O. Box 236, Croydon, Surrey. CR9 9EL

Please note readers in Southern Africa write to:
Independant Book Services P.T.Y., Postbag X3010, Randburg 2125, S. Africa

YES! Please send me 4 free Mills & Boon Romances and my free tote bag – and reserve a Reader Service Subscription for me. If I decide to subscribe I shall receive 6 new Romances every month as soon as they come off the presses for £7.50, together with a FREE monthly newsletter including information on top authors and special offers, exclusively for Reader Service subscribers. There are no postage and packing charges, and I understand I may cancel or suspend my subscription at any time. If I decide not to subscribe I shall write to you within 10 days. Even if I decide not to subscribe the 4 free novels and the tote bag are mine to keep forever. I am over 18 years of age   EP20R

NAME _____
                                                          (CAPITALS PLEASE)

ADDRESS _____

_____

_____ POSTCODE _____

Mills & Boon Ltd. reserve the right to exercise discretion in granting membership. You may be mailed with other offers as a result of this application. Offer expires 31st December 1988 and is limited to one per household.
Offer applies in UK and Eire only. Overseas send for details.